Survivor Files : Day 18

Survivor Files, Volume 20

Aaron Abilene

Published by Syphon Creative, 2024.

This is a work of fiction. Similarities to real people, places, or events are entirely coincidental.

SURVIVOR FILES : DAY 18

First edition. November 4, 2024.

ISBN: 979-8227065964

Written by Aaron Abilene.

Also by Aaron Abilene

505
505
505: Resurrection

Balls
Dead Awake
Before The Dead Awake
Dead Sleep
Bulletproof Balls

Carnival Game
Full Moon Howl
Donovan
Shades of Z

Codename
The Man in The Mini Van

Deadeye

Deadeye & Friends

Cowboys Vs Aliens

Ferris

Life in Prescott

Afterlife in Love

Tragic Heart

Island

Paradise Island

The Lost Island

The Lost Island 2

The Lost Island 3

The Island 2

Pandemic

Pandemic

Prototype

Prototype

The Compound

Slacker

Slacker 2

Slacker 3

Slacker: Dead Man Walkin'

Survivor Files

Survivor Files: Day 1

Survivor Files : Day 1 Part 2

Survivor Files : Day 2

Survivor Files : On The Run

Survivor Files : Day 3

Survivor Files : Day 4

Survivor Files : Day 5

Survivor Files : Day 6

Survivor Files : Day 7

Survivor Files : Day 8

Survivor Files : Day 9

Survivor Files : Day 10

Survivor Files : Day 11

Survivor Files : Day 12

Survivor Files : Day 13

Survivor Files : Day 14

Survivor Files : Day 15

Survivor Files : Day 16

Survivor Files : Day 17

Survivor Files : Day 18

Texas

Devil Child of Texas
A Vampire in Texas

The Author
Breaking Wind
Yellow Snow
Dragon Snatch
Golden Showers
Nether Region
Evil Empire

Thomas
Quarantine
Contagion
Eradication
Isolation
Immune
Pathogen
Bloodline
Decontaminated

TPD
Trailer Park Diaries
Trailer Park Diaries 2
Trailer Park Diaries 3

Virus

Raising Hell

Zombie Bride

Zombie Bride

Zombie Bride 2

Zombie Bride 3

Standalone

The Victims of Pinocchio

A Christmas Nightmare

Pain

Fat Jesus

A Zombie's Revenge

The Headhunter

Crash

Tranq

The Island

Dog

The Quiet Man

Joe Superhero

Feral

Good Guys

Romeo and Juliet and Zombies

The Gamer

Becoming Alpha

Dead West

Small Town Blues

Shades of Z: Redux
The Gift of Death
Killer Claus
Skarred
Home Sweet Home
Alligator Allan
10 Days
Army of The Dumbest Dead
Kid
The Cult of Stupid
9 Time Felon
Slater
Bad Review: Hannah Dies
Me Again
Maurice and Me
The Family Business
Lightning Rider : Better Days
Lazy Boyz
The Sheep
Wild
The Flood
Extinction
Good Intentions
Dark Magic
Sparkles The Vampire Clown
From The Future, Stuck in The Past
Rescue
Knock Knock
Creep
Honest John
Urbex
She's Psycho
Unfinished

Neighbors
Misery, Nevada
Vicious Cycle
Relive
Romeo and Juliet: True Love Conquers All
Dead Road
Florida Man
Hunting Sarah
The Great American Zombie Novel
Carnage
Marge 3 Toes
Random Acts of Stupidity
Born Killer
The Abducted
Whiteboy
Broken Man
Graham Hiney
Bridge
15
Paper Soldiers
Zartan
The Firsts in Life
Giant Baby

Survivor Files : Day 18

Written by Aaron Abilene

The dense foliage parted silently before me as I stalked my prey, the moist earth muffling each deliberate footfall. My eyes narrowed, fixed on the hulking boar rooting through the undergrowth ahead, oblivious to its fate. The humid air clung to my skin, my every breath measured and controlled.

I notched an arrow, the polished wood smooth against calloused fingers. Muscles coiled, ready to release in a lethal strike. The boar would feed my tribe for days. A good kill. An honorable kill.

But something felt wrong. A subtle shift, like a shadow crossing the sun. An ill wind stirring the trees. My instincts prickled with unease. Danger lurked nearby, watching, waiting. The specter of death looming just out of sight.

I hesitated, the bowstring taut against my cheek. My heart drummed a quickening beat. What twisted presence defiled these sacred hunting grounds? What unnatural thing encroached upon our ancestral lands?

The boar lifted its head, catching my scent. With a grunt it bolted, crashing through the brush. My shot went wide, the arrow thudding into a tree trunk.

I stood frozen, listening intently. Only the mournful cry of a faraway bird answered. An oppressive hush smothered the forest, the chatter of life extinguished. It was as if nature itself held its breath, awaiting some unspeakable horror.

A shudder ran through me, some primal dread awakening in my bones. The creeping certainty that an ancient evil had been roused, and the world would soon tremble before its wrath. For I alone sensed the coming storm - the heavy burden of dark tidings to bear back to my unsuspecting people.

May the spirits grant me strength, to face whatever malevolent force gathered in the shadows. For I fear our idyllic existence teeters on the edge of a yawning abyss, and I alone stand guard against the coming night. The time of innocence was over. The age of blood had begun.

A twig snapped behind me, impossibly loud in the unnatural quiet. I whirled around, bow raised, a poison-tipped arrow nocked and ready. What I saw turned my blood to ice.

A grotesque figure shambled out of the shadows, its movements jerky and unnatural. Shredded remnants of hunting garb clung to its rotting flesh, and a familiar amulet hung around its neck. With dawning horror, I recognized the twisted visage of Tarou, a fellow hunter from my village.

But this was not the Tarou I knew. His once vibrant eyes were now milky and lifeless, his skin a sickly gray, pulled taut over his skull. A gaping wound marred his throat, crusted with dried blood. He stared at me with a hollow, unsettling gaze, devoid of any human recognition.

"Tarou?" I whispered, my voice trembling. "What happened to you?"

A low, guttural moan escaped his lips, a sound that sent shivers down my spine. He lurched forward, arms outstretched, fingers grasping at empty air. The stench of decay assaulted my nostrils, making my stomach churn.

This cannot be. The dead do not walk. It defies the very laws of nature.

Yet here before me stood undeniable proof of the impossible. A abomination that mocked the sanctity of life and death. A perversion of everything I held sacred.

My mind reeled, grappling with the enormity of this revelation. If Tarou had fallen victim to this unspeakable fate, what of the others?

What of my village, my family? Were they even now under attack by an army of the undead?

I must warn them. I must protect my people, at any cost.

Tarou's advance did not falter. Though he was known by all as a fellow kinsman, I know hesitated, uncertain whether to fire. The thing before me was but an empty husk, a mockery of the man I once called friend.

With a heavy heart, I drew back the bowstring, the arrow aimed at Tarou's head. My hands shook, tears blurring my vision. In this moment, I faced an impossible choice - to end the unlife of a beloved brother, or risk the lives of all I held dear.

May the spirits forgive me for what I must do.

With a whispered prayer on my lips, I released the arrow, watching as it flew true, piercing the center of Tarou's forehead. The impact sent him stumbling backward, his lifeless body crumpling to the ground in a heap of twisted limbs.

For a moment, the only sound was the pounding of my own heart, echoing in my ears like the beat of a war drum. The forest itself seemed to hold its breath, as if in silent acknowledgment of the unnatural act that had just transpired.

I stood frozen, my bow still raised, staring at the motionless form of my fallen friend. The weight of what I had done settled upon my shoulders like a heavy mantle, threatening to crush me beneath its burden.

What manner of evil is this, that it would turn brother against brother, forcing me to commit such a heinous deed?

The rustling of leaves nearby snapped me back to the present, my senses heightened by the adrenaline coursing through my veins. I scanned the undergrowth, half-expecting another undead monstrosity to emerge from the shadows.

But there was nothing. Only the eerie silence of the forest, broken by the occasional chirp of a bird or the skittering of small animals in the brush.

I lowered my bow, my arms trembling from the exertion and the weight of my actions. The gravity of the situation began to sink in, my mind reeling with the implications of what I had just witnessed.

If the dead can rise, then none of us are safe. My village, my people... they have no idea of the danger that lurks just beyond the treeline.

I knew then that I had to warn them, to prepare them for the coming storm. But how could I make them understand the magnitude of this threat? How could I convince them of the impossible truth that now haunted my every waking thought?

I must find a way. For the sake of my tribe, for the memory of Tarou and all those we have lost, I cannot fail them now.

With a heavy sigh, I retrieved my arrow from Tarou's skull, wiping the gore on the moss-covered ground. I whispered a silent prayer for his soul, hoping that in death, he would find the peace that had eluded him in life.

Then, with a heart full of dread and a mind burdened by the knowledge of the horrors to come, I turned my back on the gruesome scene and began the long trek back to my village, each step a reminder of the weight that now rested upon my shoulders.

As I moved through the dense foliage, my thoughts raced, each one more terrifying than the last. The image of Tarou's lifeless eyes, the stench of decay that clung to his rotting flesh—these things would haunt me until my dying day. But even more chilling was the realization that he would not be the last.

How many more will rise? How long before the dead outnumber the living?

I shook my head, trying to banish the morbid thoughts that threatened to overwhelm me. I had to focus on the task at hand, on finding a way to protect my people from the coming darkness.

But what can I do? I am just one man, one hunter. How can I stand against an enemy that knows no fear, no pain, no mercy?

As I grappled with these questions, a distant sound caught my attention—the rhythmic beating of drums, the joyful laughter of children. The village was close now, blissfully unaware of the horrors that lurked just beyond the horizon.

They cannot remain ignorant forever. They must be told, must be prepared for the battles to come.

But even as I resolved to share my grim discovery, a new fear took root in my heart. How would they react to the news that the dead walked among us? Would they believe me, or would they dismiss my warnings as the ravings of a madman?

I must tread carefully, must find a way to make them see the truth without inciting panic or despair.

For I knew that in the face of this unprecedented threat, our only hope lay in standing together, in facing the darkness as one. And though the road ahead would be long and fraught with peril, I was determined to lead my people through the coming storm, no matter the cost.

No matter the cost...

The words echoed in my mind as I stepped into the village, the weight of my newfound knowledge pressing down upon me like a physical burden. Around me, life went on as usual—women gossiped by the communal fire, men sharpened their spears and arrows, children played with reckless abandon. But even as I moved among them, I felt apart, isolated by the terrible truth that I alone carried.

How can I protect them when I myself am so afraid?

The thought gnawed at me, a persistent whisper of doubt that threatened to undermine my resolve. As the son of the chief, it was my duty to lead, to guide my people through whatever challenges lay ahead. But in the face of this new enemy, an enemy that defied all reason and natural law, I found myself questioning whether I was truly up to the task.

What if I fail them? What if my weakness dooms us all?

I shook my head, banishing the dark thoughts with an effort of will. There was no room for self-doubt, not now, not with so much at stake. I had to be strong, had to find a way to unite my people against the coming storm.

But first, I needed time—time to think, to plan, to devise a strategy that would give us a fighting chance. And so, with a heavy heart, I made my way to my father's hut, determined to keep my discovery a secret for just a little while longer.

Forgive me, father, for the lies I must tell. But I cannot risk spreading panic, not until I have a plan.

As I ducked through the low doorway, I could only pray that the ancestors would guide me, that they would grant me the wisdom and strength to lead my people through the dark days ahead. For in the face of the risen dead, we would need every ounce of courage and cunning we could muster if we hoped to survive.

The village hummed with life, blissfully unaware of the horrors lurking just beyond the treeline. Children's laughter echoed through the air, mingling with the rhythmic pounding of pestles as women prepared the evening meal. In the central clearing, a group of elders sat cross-legged, their weathered faces illuminated by the flickering light of a bonfire as they shared stories of our people's past.

I watched them, my heart aching with the weight of my secret. How could I shatter their peace, their sense of security? How could I tell them that the dead now walked among us, hungry for the flesh of the living?

No, not yet. I need more time.

I forced myself to join them, to sit and listen as the tales of our ancestors washed over me. The fire crackled and danced, casting eerie shadows across the clearing, and for a moment, I could almost forget the nightmare that awaited us.

But then, the wind shifted, carrying with it the faint scent of decay, and I felt a chill run down my spine. *They're coming*, a voice whispered in my mind. *The dead are coming, and we are not ready.*

I clenched my fists, my resolve hardening like tempered steel. I would not let my people fall, not without a fight. I would find a way to protect them, to lead them through this darkness, no matter the cost.

As the night wore on and the village began to settle into sleep, I slipped away, my mind racing with half-formed plans and desperate schemes. I would need weapons, defenses, a way to train my people to fight against an enemy they could scarcely comprehend.

But most of all, I would need their trust, their unwavering loyalty. For only together could we hope to stand against the rising tide of the undead.

I am Maikoru, son of the chief, I told myself, my jaw set with grim determination. *And I will not let my people fall.*

With that thought burning in my mind, I set to work, the weight of my people's fate resting heavily upon my shoulders as the night deepened around me.

The thick tangle of vines and broad leaves ensnared my senses as I crept through the undergrowth. The calls and cries of birds and beasts echoed around me, but I paid them no heed. My focus was singular - find game to bring back to the village. That was my purpose out here, amidst the green. My purpose before all this began, before the dead began to walk.

My eyes traced the path ahead, seeking signs - a hoofprint, a broken twig, the bent grass where some creature had passed. My nostrils flared, trying to catch a scent on the heavy, humid air. Ears strained to hear the crunch of dead leaves, a snort, a growl, anything. All my senses were open, drinking in the rainforest, alert for my prey.

A rustle. There. To the right. I froze, muscles tensing, heartbeat thundering in my ears. Hand inched towards my bow. Fingers curled around the wood, an extension of my being. I waited, poised, a jaguar ready to spring. The rustling came again, closer. Louder. Something approached. Time stretched, seconds into eternities.

My breath came shallow and fast. Sweat beaded on my brow, rolling down like the tears of the dead. Was it them? The cursed ones? The horror that now stalked these woods, relentless, unnatural. No. I would not let that old fear master me. I was Maikoru! The greatest hunter of the—

Another rustle shattered my thoughts, jolting me back to the now. I crouched lower, eyes narrowed, pulse racing. What emerged from those fronds would meet the wrath of my bow. The strength of my arm. The courage in my heart. I would not run. I would not cower. Let it come, beast or demon! Maikoru fears no evil now. Only the faces that haunt his dreams...

A grotesque shape lurched from the foliage. Jerky, spasmodic movements, like a macabre marionette dancing on broken strings. Dead eyes stared, milky and unseeing. Gray flesh hung in tatters from jutting bones. The stench of decay slammed into me, choking, overwhelming.

Horror crushed my chest like a vice. No. Not this. Anything but this. The nightmare we thought we'd left behind, rotting in the ruins of the old world. Yet here it stood. Undead. Undying. Relentless as the turning of the earth. As inevitable as the sins of our past.

Unbidden, a moan of despair rose in my throat. "No, no, no..." Senseless prayers to uncaring gods. The thing that was once human stumbled closer, jaw slack, arms raised. Hungry. Soulless. A perversion of life itself.

With trembling hands, I notched an arrow. The shaft was slick with poison, deadly and merciless. My fingers found the bowstring, an old friend, a well-worn path. I drew it back, muscles screaming with tension. Focused my aim on that horrid, lurching skull. One shot. One kill. As I'd done a thousand times before.

But this was no beast of the forest. No prey to be honored. This was damnation in mortal form. The sins of our hubris, come back to devour us. As we deserved. As I deserved, for the blood on my hands, the screams that still echoed...

No. Focus, Maikoru. One shot. Set them free. Set yourself free. My fingers tensed, bowstring cutting into flesh. I sighted down the arrow, seeing only my target. My torment. My penance. And with grim finality, I let fly the arrow that would damn me anew.

The arrow sliced through fetid air, a whisper of death on rotting winds. For a heartbeat, the world held its breath. Then, with sickening finality, it struck true - a perfect shot, piercing decayed skull and rancid brain. The creature jerked, spasmed, an obscene marionette with severed strings. And fell, crumpling to the forest floor with a hollow thud.

I lowered my bow, arms numb, chest heaving. Stared at the twisted remains, bile rising in my throat. It was done. I had ended it. As I always did. As I always must.

But there was no triumph in it. No joy or glory. Only the bitter ashes of necessity, choking my heart. Another lost soul, condemned by my hand. Another ghost to haunt my steps, whispering accusations in the dark watches of the night.

"Forgive me," I breathed, to the unhearing corpse. Hollow words, undeserved. Forgiveness was not for the likes of me. Not anymore. Not after all I had done. All I had failed to do.

I turned away, shoulders bowed beneath the weight of my sins. Retraced my steps through the clinging vines, the grasping shadows. Each footfall echoed with recrimination, dragging at my heels.

Drawing me inexorably back. Back to the village. Back to the faces that looked to me for hope. For salvation.

Fools, all of us. There was no salvation to be had. Not in this blighted world of ruin and regret. We were as doomed as the shambling horror I had felled. As doomed as the dreams of the past, crumbling to dust in the cold light of day.

But still, I walked on. Still, I carried the burden they thrust upon me. The mantle of leadership, of guardianship, that I had never asked for. Never wanted. And with each step, I felt myself wither further. Felt my soul crumble beneath the weight of their belief.

For in the end, it would not be the undead that destroyed me. But the living, with their fragile hopes and faithless prayers. The innocents I was sworn to protect...even as they dragged me into the abyss.

The village gate loomed before me, a portal to a world I no longer recognized. A world where the line between the living and the dead had blurred, leaving only uncertainty and dread in its wake. I paused, hand resting on the weathered wood, feeling the weight of the responsibility that lay beyond.

They would look to me for answers, for guidance. They would expect me to lead them through this nightmare, to find a way to keep them safe. But how could I protect them when I could barely keep my own demons at bay?

I closed my eyes, drew in a shuddering breath. Tried to steel myself for what lay ahead. But there was no strength left in me. No courage, no conviction. Only the bitter taste of failure, the acrid stench of my own fear.

"Maikoru?" a voice called out, tentative, afraid. "What happened out there? Did you find anything?"

I opened my eyes, saw the faces of the villagers gathering around me. Saw the hope in their eyes, the desperate need for reassurance. And I knew that I could not give it to them.

"We're in danger," I said, my voice flat, emotionless. "The undead are coming. And there's nothing we can do to stop them."

A murmur rippled through the crowd, a rising tide of fear and disbelief. I saw the accusation in their eyes, the unspoken question: How could I, their protector, their savior, have failed them so utterly?

But I had no answers for them. No comfort to offer. Only the cold, hard truth of our impending doom.

"We must prepare," I said, forcing the words past the lump in my throat. "Fortify the village, gather what weapons we can. And pray to whatever gods may still listen that we can hold out long enough to...to..."

But I could not finish the sentence. Could not give voice to the hopelessness that consumed me. For in that moment, I knew with a terrible certainty that there would be no escape. No reprieve.

We were already dead. We just didn't know it yet.

The weight of my words hung heavy in the air, suffocating in their finality. I watched as the villagers exchanged glances, their faces etched with a mixture of disbelief and growing despair. Some shook their heads, unwilling to accept the truth, while others clutched at their loved ones, tears streaming down their faces.

"Maikoru," a voice called out, trembling with fear. "What can we do? How can we possibly survive this?"

I looked into their eyes, saw the same hopelessness that threatened to consume me. But I knew I could not let it show. I had to be strong, for them. For all of us.

"We fight," I said, my voice steady despite the turmoil raging inside me. "We use every resource at our disposal, every ounce of strength we possess. We do not go quietly into the night."

A murmur of agreement rippled through the crowd, a flicker of determination igniting in their eyes. I saw the warriors step forward, their jaws set with grim resolve. They knew, as I did, that our chances were slim. But they would not abandon their duty, their sacred oath to protect the village at all costs.

As the villagers dispersed to begin their preparations, I turned away, my shoulders sagging under the weight of my own guilt. I had brought this upon them, with my arrogance, my foolish belief that I could keep them safe. And now, I had condemned them all to a fate worse than death.

But even as despair threatened to engulf me, I felt a flicker of something else, buried deep within my soul. A spark of defiance, of stubborn refusal to surrender. I may have failed them once, but I would not do so again.

I would fight, until my last breath, to give them a chance at survival. And maybe, just maybe, in doing so, I could find some measure of redemption for my sins.

As the sun began its descent, casting an eerie orange glow over the village, I found myself pacing restlessly, my mind churning with dark thoughts. The weight of responsibility pressed down upon me, suffocating in its intensity. I had brought this nightmare to our doorstep, and now it fell to me to lead us through the coming storm.

I watched as the villagers worked tirelessly to fortify our defenses, their faces etched with a mixture of fear and determination. They erected barricades from whatever materials they could find, sharpened stakes and fashioned crude weapons from tools of daily life. It was a pitiful sight, a testament to our desperation.

In the midst of the preparations, a young warrior approached me, his eyes wide with barely concealed terror. "Maikoru," he whispered, his voice trembling, "do you really think we can survive this?"

I met his gaze, my own eyes haunted by the weight of my sins. "I don't know," I admitted, my voice low and hoarse. "But we have no choice but to try."

The warrior nodded, his jaw clenching with resolve. "We will follow you, Maikoru. To whatever end."

His words struck me like a physical blow, the loyalty and trust they conveyed both humbling and terrifying. I knew I didn't deserve it, not after what I had done. But I also knew that I could not let them down, not again.

As night fell, an unnatural stillness settled over the village, broken only by the occasional whisper of the wind through the trees. I stood at the edge of the perimeter, my bow clutched tightly in my hands, my senses straining for any sign of the approaching horde.

And then, in the distance, I heard it. The shuffling of feet, the guttural moans of the undead. They were coming, an unstoppable force of hunger and decay, and we were all that stood between them and oblivion.

I turned to face the village, my voice ringing out in the darkness. "They're here," I said, my words heavy with finality. "May the gods have mercy on us all."

A shudder rippled through the gathered warriors, their faces pale in the flickering torchlight. I could see the fear in their eyes, the same fear that gnawed at my own gut, but there was something else there too. A fierce determination, a willingness to fight and die for what they held dear.

"We stand together," I said, my voice steady despite the tremors that wracked my body. "We fight as one, and we do not falter."

The warriors nodded, their grip tightening on their weapons. I could feel their energy, their resolve, and it bolstered my own flagging courage.

"Remember what we're fighting for," I continued, my gaze sweeping over the assembled tribe. "Our homes, our families, our very way of life. We will not let the undead take that from us."

A murmur of agreement swept through the crowd, and I felt a surge of pride. These were my people, and I would not let them down.

But even as I spoke, I could feel the weight of my own secrets pressing down on me, the knowledge of what I had done and what I had become. I had brought this upon us, through my own weakness and folly, and now we all had to pay the price.

The moans of the undead grew louder, closer, and I knew that the time for words was over. I turned to face the approaching horde, my bow at the ready, my heart pounding in my chest.

"For the village!" I cried, my voice ringing out over the din. "For our survival!"

And with that, we charged forward, a small but determined force against the relentless tide of death. The battle had begun, and only the gods knew how it would end.

As the undead horde approached, their shambling steps and guttural moans filling the air, I felt a chill run down my spine. The village had sprung into action, following my lead, but doubt began to creep into my mind. What if our defenses weren't enough? What if I had led my people to their doom?

I shook my head, pushing those thoughts aside. There was no time for self-doubt, not now. I had to be strong, for my people and for myself.

The first wave of zombies crashed against our barricades, their rotting hands clawing at the wooden stakes. The warriors beside me let out a fierce battle cry, thrusting their spears forward, impaling the creatures. The air was thick with the stench of decay and the coppery tang of blood.

I notched an arrow, my fingers trembling slightly as I took aim. The zombie in my sights was once a man, a member of our tribe. His face was twisted in a grotesque snarl, his eyes vacant and lifeless. I hesitated, a pang of remorse tearing at my heart.

"Maikoru!" Tanaka, one of the elder warriors, shouted. "You must strike!"

His words jolted me back to reality. I released the arrow, watching as it found its mark, piercing the zombie's skull. The creature crumpled to the ground, unmoving.

"Don't let them get inside your head," Tanaka warned, his eyes meeting mine. "They're not who they once were. They're nothing more than shells now, filled with an insatiable hunger."

I nodded, steeling myself against the onslaught. We fought for what seemed like an eternity, the undead pressing against our defenses, relentless in their assault. My arms ached from the strain of firing arrow after arrow, my mind numb from the ceaseless carnage.

But even as we fought, I couldn't shake the feeling that this was only the beginning. The undead had found us, and they would not rest until every last one of us was either dead or turned.

As the battle raged on, I caught glimpses of the villagers, their faces etched with determination and fear. They trusted me to lead them through this nightmare, to keep them safe. But with each passing moment, I felt that trust slipping away, replaced by the cold realization that I might not be the savior they believed me to be.

The weight of my past, of the secrets I kept hidden, seemed to grow heavier with each fallen zombie. I had brought this upon us, and now we all had to face the consequences.

The village fought on, our resolve unwavering even as our numbers dwindled. We would not go quietly into the night, not while there was still breath in our bodies and fire in our hearts.

But deep down, I knew that this was only the beginning of our struggle against the undead. The true test of our survival was yet to come, and I feared that my own demons might be our undoing.

The morning sun filtered through the dense canopy, dappling the village in a tranquil glow. Birds chattered overhead, their melodic songs weaving through the hum of insects. Children's laughter echoed from the huts as they chased each other, blissfully unaware of the nightmare that was about to unfold.

I sat on my porch, sipping a cup of strong herbal tea, the steam curling around my face. A sense of unease twisted in my gut, though

I couldn't say why. Something felt off, like a discordant note in the symphony of the rainforest.

Then I heard it - a guttural moan that sent icy tendrils down my spine. It rose in volume, joined by other unearthly groans and snarls. The birds fell silent. Even the insects seemed to hold their breath.

I leapt to my feet just as the first zombie stumbled into view at the edge of the village. Its flesh hung in ragged strips from its bones, maggots writhing in the putrid meat. Clouded eyes rolled in its skull, fixing on the nearest hut with predatory focus.

"Zombies! To arms!" I cried, terror and adrenaline surging through my veins.

All around, villagers emerged from their homes, some still rubbing sleep from their eyes. Confusion rapidly morphed into horror as more zombies poured out of the trees, a macabre tide of rotting flesh and gnashing teeth. Panic erupted, people screaming and running in all directions.

I grabbed the machete at my belt, the weight familiar and reassuring in my grip. Akiko appeared at my side, her own blade glinting in the sun. Her face was pale but determined, dark eyes glinting with fear and resolve.

"It's really happening," she whispered, voice trembling slightly. "Everything we feared..."

I swallowed hard, trying to master the terror clawing at my throat. The stench of decay was overwhelming, making my gorge rise.

"We'll get through this together," I said, injecting more confidence than I felt into my tone. "Let's go."

Side by side, Akiko and I charged forward to meet the horde, our war cries joining the cacophony of shrieks and moans that shattered the peace of our village, knowing that this day would change everything, and that our idyllic existence had come to a brutal end. The nightmares we'd held at bay for so long had finally broken free.

I rallied the warriors with hoarse shouts, my machete slicing through putrid flesh and bone. We formed a defensive line, desperation lending strength to our blows as we fought to push back the relentless tide of undead.

Beside me, Akiko was a whirlwind of steel, her blade flashing in the sun as she cut down zombie after zombie. Blood and gore spattered her face, but she never faltered, never slowed. Pride and love surged through me even as dread coiled in my gut.

The villagers fought with everything they had, wielding fishing spears, sharpened sticks, and heavy stones. Some took to the trees, raining down arrows and darts tipped with poison frogs' venom. Others laid traps, guiding the zombies into pits lined with sharpened stakes.

But for every monster we felled, two more seemed to take its place. They came at us with single-minded hunger, heedless of injury, driven only by the insatiable need to feed. Slowly, inexorably, they pushed us back.

"Fall back to the center of the village!" I roared over the clamor of battle. "Defend the heart of our home!"

We gave ground grudgingly, fighting for every inch. I saw friends and neighbors fall, heard their screams cut short as they were dragged down and torn apart. Each loss was a knife to my heart, but I couldn't stop, couldn't let myself feel it yet.

At the village center, we made our stand around the ancient tree that had watched over us for generations. Its vast canopy shielded us as we regrouped, tending to the wounded and catching our breath. But the reprieve was short-lived.

The zombies swarmed in from all sides, a sea of grasping hands and snapping jaws. We met them head-on, fighting with the desperate strength of cornered prey. The air was thick with the copper tang of blood and the stench of death.

I lost myself in the rhythm of battle, my world narrowing to the next swing of my blade, the next rotting corpse to put down. Time lost all meaning; there was only the fight, the struggle to survive, to protect those I loved.

But deep down, I knew it wasn't enough. We were too few, the enemy too many. Sooner or later, we would falter, and the village would fall. The only question was how long we could hold out, and how many we could save before the end.

As if in answer to my darkest thoughts, a scream cut through the din, high and piercing. I knew that voice, would know it anywhere. Cold horror flooded my veins as I turned, already knowing what I would see.

Akiko...

My feet carried me toward that terrible cry, heedless of the danger. I cut down the zombies in my path with savage efficiency, desperate to reach her. The sight that greeted me when I arrived at our home will haunt me until my dying day.

Akiko stood in the doorway, her back to me, facing down a horde of the undead. She fought like a tigress, all grace and fury, the very image of the warrior I fell in love with. But for every zombie she felled, two more took its place. They pressed in, relentless, drawn by the promise of living flesh.

I lunged forward, bellowing her name, but I was too late. A zombie slipped past her guard, its teeth sinking deep into her forearm. Her scream of pain and horror mingled with my own anguished cry. I reached her side, cleaving the monster's head from its shoulders, but the damage was done.

Akiko sagged against me, her face ashen. I held her close, my mind reeling, refusing to accept the terrible reality. This couldn't be happening, not to her, not to us. We had survived so much, overcome every obstacle. Surely fate couldn't be so cruel.

But even as I clung to her, I watched the light in her eyes begin to fade, replaced by a dull, vacant hunger. The warmth leeched from her skin, leaving her cold and clammy in my arms. She stirred, her movements jerky and unnatural, a low moan issuing from her throat.

"No," I whispered, my voice breaking. "Akiko, please, don't leave me. I can't do this without you."

But she was already gone, the woman I loved consumed by the insatiable hunger of the undead. In her place was a monster wearing her face, a twisted mockery of everything she had been. My heart shattered, the pieces ground to dust beneath the weight of my grief and despair.

I stood, my legs trembling, as Akiko-no, the creature that had once been Akiko-staggered to her feet. She lurched towards me, her arms outstretched, fingers grasping. I stumbled back, my mind reeling, my heart in tatters.

"Akiko, please," I begged, knowing it was futile. "It's me, Maikoru. Your husband. Don't you remember?"

But there was no recognition in those lifeless eyes, no trace of the love and warmth that had once filled them. Only hunger, raw and all-consuming, driving her forward.

Around us, the battle raged on, the screams of the dying mingling with the guttural moans of the undead. I knew I had to act, had to protect what remained of my people. But how could I raise my hand against the woman I loved, the one who had been my heart and soul for so long?

Akiko stumbled closer, her jaws snapping, her fingers clawing at my skin. I danced back, my weapon heavy in my hand. Tears blurred my vision, my breath coming in ragged gasps. I had to end this, had to release her from this torment. But the thought of striking her down, of watching the light leave her eyes forever, was more than I could bear.

"Forgive me," I whispered, my voice raw with anguish. "I love you, Akiko. I always will."

With a cry that tore from the depths of my shattered soul, I raised my weapon and brought it down, the blade cleaving through flesh and bone. Akiko crumpled, her body falling at my feet, the hunger in her eyes extinguished forever.

I sank to my knees, my weapon slipping from numb fingers. I gathered her into my arms, cradling her lifeless form against my chest. Sobs wracked my body, tears streaming down my face. The world around me faded away, the sounds of battle receding into the distance. In that moment, there was only my grief, raw and all-consuming, and the knowledge that I would never again feel the warmth of her touch, the comfort of her presence.

But even in the depths of my despair, I knew I had to go on. For the sake of my people, for the memory of the woman I had loved and lost. I would fight, I would lead, I would do whatever it took to ensure our survival in this cruel, unforgiving world.

With a final, anguished kiss to Akiko's cold forehead, I laid her down gently and rose to my feet. The weight of my grief was a physical thing, pressing down on my shoulders, but I bore it with grim determination. For Akiko, for my people, I would endure. I would find a way to carry on, even in the face of this unimaginable loss.

I turned to face the remaining villagers, their faces etched with fear and sorrow. They looked to me for guidance, for strength, and I knew I could not let them down. Not now, not ever.

"My friends," I said, my voice hoarse with emotion, "we cannot stay here. The undead will return, and we cannot hope to withstand another assault. We must leave this place, our home, and seek safety in the depths of the rainforest."

Murmurs of dissent rippled through the crowd, but I pressed on. "I know it is a difficult decision, to abandon all that we have ever known. But we have no choice. To stay here is to invite death, to condemn ourselves to a fate worse than any we could imagine."

I looked into their eyes, seeing the fear, the uncertainty, but also the glimmer of hope. "We are strong," I said, my voice growing in strength and conviction. "We are resilient. We have faced hardships before, and we have overcome them. Together, we will find a way to survive, to build a new life for ourselves in the heart of the rainforest."

Slowly, hesitantly at first, then with growing resolve, the villagers began to nod. They gathered their belongings, their weapons, their meager supplies, and prepared to leave the only home they had ever known.

As we set out into the unknown, the weight of my grief still heavy upon me, I felt a flicker of something else, something I had not felt in a long time: hope. Hope that we could find a way to survive, to thrive, even in the face of unspeakable horror. Hope that Akiko's sacrifice would not be in vain, that her memory would live on in the hearts and minds of our people.

And so, with a heavy heart and a determined spirit, I led my people into the depths of the rainforest, into an uncertain future, but one that held the promise of a new beginning, a chance to start anew in a world gone mad.

I turned for one last look at the village that had been our sanctuary, our home, for as long as I could remember. The huts stood silent and empty, their thatched roofs smoldering from the fires that had raged during the battle. The once vibrant gardens lay trampled and ruined, the crops that had sustained us now nothing more than rotting remnants.

But it was the bodies that haunted me most—the bodies of friends, of family, of those I had sworn to protect. They lay where they had fallen, their faces frozen in final expressions of terror and agony. And among them, the body of my beloved Akiko, her once beautiful features now twisted and grotesque, a cruel mockery of the woman I had loved.

I forced myself to look away, to turn my back on the past and face the uncertain future that lay ahead. The rainforest loomed before us, dark and foreboding, its secrets hidden beneath a canopy of leaves and vines. It was a place of danger, of untold horrors lurking in the shadows, but it was also our only hope, our only chance at survival.

As we made our way into the dense undergrowth, the sounds of the village faded behind us, replaced by the eerie silence of the jungle. Each step took us further from the life we had known, from the memories that haunted us, but also closer to the promise of a new beginning.

I could feel the eyes of my people upon me, their hope and their fear mingling in the heavy air. They looked to me for guidance, for strength, for the courage to face the unknown. And so, I squared my shoulders and set my jaw, determined to be the leader they needed, to guide them through the darkness and into the light.

But even as I walked, the weight of my grief threatened to overwhelm me, the memory of Akiko's lifeless body seared into my mind. I knew that I would carry that image with me forever, a constant reminder of the price we had paid, of the sacrifices we had made.

And yet, even in the depths of my despair, I clung to the hope that had taken root in my heart. The hope that we could find a way to survive, to build a new life for ourselves in the heart of the rainforest. The hope that Akiko's memory would live on, a guiding light in the darkness, a reminder of the love and the strength that had once been ours.

And so, we pressed on, into the unknown, into the future, our footsteps echoing through the silence of the jungle, a testament to our resilience, our determination, and our unwavering spirit in the face of the unspeakable.

The dense foliage seemed to swallow us whole as we ventured deeper into the heart of the rainforest, the cries of exotic birds and the rustling of unseen creatures filling the air. I led the way, machete in hand, hacking through the thick undergrowth with a fierce determination, my mind focused solely on the task at hand.

Behind me, the villagers followed in a single file, their eyes wide with fear and uncertainty. I could hear their whispered prayers, their pleas for protection from the spirits of the forest. But I knew that no amount of prayer could save us from the horrors that lurked in the shadows.

"Maikoru," a voice called out, breaking the eerie silence. I turned to see Takeshi, my closest friend and confidant, his face etched with concern. "We need to find shelter, a place to rest and regroup."

I nodded, my eyes scanning the dense foliage for any sign of a suitable location. "There," I said, pointing to a small clearing just ahead. "We'll make camp there for the night."

As we set about erecting makeshift shelters from the broad leaves and sturdy branches of the surrounding trees, I couldn't shake the feeling that we were being watched, that something dark and sinister was lurking just beyond the edge of the clearing.

"Do you think they'll find us here?" Takeshi asked, his voice low and hesitant.

I shook my head, my gaze fixed on the darkening sky above. "I don't know," I admitted, my words heavy with the weight of uncertainty. "But we can't afford to let our guard down, not even for a moment."

As the night closed in around us, I settled into an uneasy sleep, my dreams haunted by visions of Akiko, her lifeless eyes staring back at me from the depths of my subconscious. And even as I woke, gasping for breath, the sound of distant moans carried on the wind, a chilling reminder of the danger that lurked just beyond the treeline.

I strode through the village, my heart hammering against my ribs. The huts loomed around me, their shadows seeming to reach out with grasping fingers. I needed to find Osamu. Only he could guide us now, with the horrors that lurked beyond the trees.

There. Beneath the gnarled branches of the ancient kapok tree. Osamu sat cross-legged, his wrinkled face as still as carved wood. As if sensing my approach, his eyes opened, fixing me with a penetrating stare. He beckoned with one bony finger.

I hurried over and knelt before him, the rich scent of soil and moss filling my nostrils. "Wise one, I seek your counsel. A darkness is coming for us all. I fear we cannot stand against it."

Osamu regarded me, ancient eyes swirling with knowledge accumulated over countless moons. Moons unstained by the evil that now crept forth to smother the world in shadow.

"You were right to come, Maikoru," he said, voice crackling like dry leaves. "I have long sensed the malevolent forces gathering. Abominations that should never rise again stir from ageless slumber, hungering for living flesh."

A chill shivered down my spine at his words, though the humid air pressed against my skin. The knowing in Osamu's eyes reflected my own dread, magnified a hundredfold by his decades.

He knew. He knew the enormity of what we faced. The responsibility crashed over me, threatening to drive me to my knees. How could I lead my people against such an unfathomable evil?

As if reading my thoughts, Osamu leaned forward, laying a weathered hand on my shoulder. "You must be their strength, Maikoru. Their light in the darkness. I will share what wisdom I can to guide your path."

I swallowed against the tightness in my throat and nodded. "Tell me, wise one. Tell me how to save our people."

Osamu's grip tightened, his eyes boring into mine with an intensity that made me want to look away. But I couldn't. Not now. Not when the fate of our tribe hung in the balance.

"The undead fear not pain, nor hunger, nor reason," he began, his voice taking on a rhythmic cadence that seemed to echo through my bones. "They are a pestilence, a blight upon the land. Their touch corrupts, their hunger insatiable. They will not stop until every last living soul is consumed."

Images flashed through my mind, unbidden. Rotting corpses shambling through our village, their moans mingling with the screams of the dying. The stench of decay and the metallic tang of blood. Our people, torn apart and devoured.

I shuddered, bile rising in my throat. "How do we stop them?"

"You cannot meet them head-on," Osamu warned, his voice barely above a whisper. "They are too many, too relentless. You must be like the jaguar stalking its prey. Swift, silent, and precise."

He leaned closer, his breath hot against my ear. "Strike at their heads, for that is where their unnatural life resides. Crush the skull, sever the spine, and they will fall. Fire, too, can be an ally. The flames will cleanse the corruption from their flesh."

I nodded, committing his words to memory. "What else?"

"You must lead your people to higher ground," Osamu continued, his gaze distant as if seeing things I could not. "The undead do not tire, do not rest. You must use the land to your advantage. Seek out places where they cannot reach, where you can defend and fortify."

His words painted a grim picture, but one that offered a glimmer of hope. A chance, however slim, for survival. For a future.

I met Osamu's gaze, my resolve hardening like tempered steel. "I will do whatever it takes to save our people."

A flicker of pride danced in Osamu's ancient eyes, mingling with the sorrow that seemed to be his constant companion. "I have seen the strength within you, Maikoru. The courage that burns bright, even in the face of unspeakable darkness."

He placed a gnarled hand on my shoulder, his grip surprisingly firm. "You are the one who will lead our people to safety. The one who will ensure that our legacy survives, even as the world crumbles around us."

I swallowed hard, the weight of his words settling upon my shoulders like a physical burden. "But what if I fail? What if I'm not strong enough?"

Osamu's gaze bore into mine, unwavering. "You are stronger than you know, Maikoru. The blood of warriors flows through your veins. The spirit of our ancestors guides your every step."

He leaned back, his voice taking on a distant quality. "I have seen the signs, the omens that speak of a great trial to come. A battle that will determine the fate of our people. And you, Maikoru, will be at the center of it all."

My heart raced, a mixture of fear and exhilaration coursing through my veins. The future stretched out before me, a twisting path shrouded in shadows and uncertainty. But in that moment, I knew that I could not turn away. I could not abandon my people, my family.

I met Osamu's gaze once more, my voice steady despite the tremors that wracked my body. "I will do whatever it takes," I repeated, the words a solemn vow. "I will lead our people to safety, no matter the cost."

Osamu nodded, a faint smile tugging at the corners of his weathered lips. "Then go, Maikoru. Gather your strength, for the journey ahead will be long and treacherous. But know that you do not walk alone. The spirits of our ancestors will be with you, every step of the way."

As I turned to leave, my mind reeling with the enormity of the task before me, Osamu's voice drifted after me, a haunting whisper that seemed to echo through the very fabric of my being.

"Remember, Maikoru. In the face of darkness, it is the light within that will guide you home."

The weight of Osamu's words hung heavy upon my shoulders as I trudged back through the village, my footsteps echoing hollowly in the eerie stillness. The air itself seemed to hold its breath, as if the very world was waiting, watching, to see what I would do next.

I found myself drawn to the central fire pit, where the embers of last night's blaze still glowed faintly, a reminder of the warmth and comfort that had once been. I sank to my knees beside it, my fingers tracing idly through the ashes, as if searching for some hidden message, some clue that would guide me forward.

But there was nothing. Only the cold, hard truth of what lay ahead.

I closed my eyes, letting the memories wash over me. The laughter of children, the soft murmur of voices around the fire, the sense of belonging that had once been so strong. All of it, gone now, swept away by the relentless tide of the undead.

A soft rustle behind me snapped me back to the present, and I turned to see Akiko, one of the pregnant women, standing hesitantly at the edge of the clearing. Her belly was swollen with new life, a cruel contrast to the death that surrounded us.

"Maikoru," she whispered, her voice trembling. "What are we going to do?"

I rose slowly to my feet, dusting the ashes from my hands. "We're going to survive," I said, my voice sounding strange and distant to my own ears. "We're going to leave this place, find somewhere safe."

Akiko's eyes widened, fear and uncertainty warring in their depths. "But how? Where will we go?"

I shook my head, the weight of responsibility settling heavily upon my shoulders. "I don't know," I admitted. "But we can't stay here. We have to try."

I turned to face the rest of the village, my voice rising to carry across the silent huts and empty streets. "Gather what you can," I called out. "Food, water, weapons. We leave at dawn."

As the survivors began to stir, their faces etched with grief and desperation, I felt a flicker of doubt, a whisper of fear that perhaps I was leading them all to their doom.

But then I remembered Osamu's words, the quiet strength in his voice as he spoke of the sacrifices that had been made, the battles that had been fought. And I knew that I could not falter, could not let my own doubts and fears consume me.

For I was their leader now, the one they looked to for guidance and hope. And I would not let them down, no matter the cost.

As the sun dipped below the horizon, painting the sky in hues of blood red and deepening shadows, I made my way through the village, my footsteps heavy and purposeful. The survivors watched me pass, their eyes haunted and hollow, their faces gaunt with hunger and fear.

I stopped before each of them, meeting their gazes with a steadiness I did not feel, speaking words of encouragement and reassurance. "We will find a way," I promised, my voice low and fierce. "We will not let the undead claim us."

Some nodded, their expressions grim with determination, while others wept silently, their shoulders shaking with the weight of their grief. I understood their pain, felt it like a knife in my own heart, but I could not let it consume me, could not let it cloud my judgment or weaken my resolve.

For I knew that our survival depended on our ability to act, to move swiftly and decisively in the face of the approaching horde. And so I pushed forward, gathering supplies and weapons, organizing the strongest among us into a defensive perimeter around the village.

As the night deepened and the shadows lengthened, I found myself standing at the edge of the village, staring out into the darkness of the rainforest beyond. The weight of Osamu's words echoed in my mind, the knowledge of what we must do, of the sacrifices we must make.

And yet, even as I steeled myself for the journey ahead, I felt a flicker of doubt, a whisper of uncertainty that perhaps I was not strong enough, not wise enough to lead my people to safety.

But then I thought of the lives that depended on me, the unborn children and the elderly, the wounded and the weak. And I knew that I could not falter, could not let my own fears and doubts consume me.

For I was their leader now, their protector and their guide. And I would do whatever it took to ensure their survival, to lead them through the darkness and into the light beyond.

With a final glance back at the village that had been my home for so long, I turned and stepped into the shadows of the rainforest, the weight of my people's lives heavy upon my shoulders, and the echoes of Osamu's wisdom ringing in my ears.

The rustle of leaves and the crunch of undergrowth filled the air as we moved deeper into the heart of the rainforest. The moon's pale light filtered through the dense canopy, casting an eerie glow upon our procession. I could hear the muffled sobs of those who had left their homes, their lives, behind.

"Stay close," I whispered, my voice barely audible above the symphony of the night. "We must be swift and silent."

I glanced back at the faces of my people, their eyes wide with fear and uncertainty. The pregnant women cradled their swollen bellies, their steps heavy with the burden of new life. The warriors, once proud and strong, now moved with a hunted wariness, their weapons clutched tightly in their hands.

As we pressed on, the forest seemed to close in around us, the shadows deepening and the air growing thick with the scent of decay. I could feel the weight of the undead's presence, the knowledge that they lurked just beyond the reach of our torchlight.

And yet, even as the fear threatened to overwhelm me, I clung to the memories of Osamu's words, to the wisdom he had imparted in those final moments. I knew that our survival depended on my ability to lead, to make the hard choices that would keep us alive.

But with each step, I could feel the burden of my past sins weighing down upon me, the ghosts of those I had failed whispering in my ear. The blood on my hands seemed to glisten in the moonlight, a reminder of the lives I had taken, the choices I had made.

And I wondered, as we moved ever deeper into the heart of darkness, if I was truly worthy of the trust my people had placed in me, if I had the strength to lead them to a future beyond the shadow of the undead.

The jungle envelops us as I lead our ragged band deeper into its humid embrace. With each squelching step, the fevered chatter of unseen beasts pricks at my skin. The weight of their lives presses down on me, a burden I cannot set aside. Not after all we've endured.

Riku shadows me, coiled and ready to strike. His katana, our last defense against the horrors that stalk us, glints in the filtered light. "We can't keep running forever," he says, his voice scraping raw.

I meet his weary gaze, seeing in it an echo of my own haunted reflection. "No. But we'll run as long as we must. For them." My eyes flicker to the women trailing behind us, their swollen bellies a reminder of the innocence we still cling to. The innocence we fight to protect.

A shrill cry pierces the air and Riku's hand clutches his weapon, white-knuckled. I taste the tang of fear on my tongue but force my legs to keep moving, to propel us forward into the unknown.

The ghosts of those we've lost dog our steps, whispering accusations that burrow into my mind. I shut them out, focusing only on the path ahead, on the next bend, the next breath. Survival is all that matters now. Survival, and the promise of new life cradled within the women who follow.

Redemption is a distant dream, but still, we press on. Through the shadows and the suffocating heat. Through the gnawing hunger and the crippling fatigue. We press on, because there is no other choice. No other path but forward, into the maw of the jungle and whatever fate awaits.

The path narrows, the dense foliage pressing in on either side like grasping hands. My heart hammers against my ribs as we approach the ravine, a jagged scar cutting through the earth. I pause at the edge, peering down into the yawning depths, the distant sound of rushing water echoing up from the shadows.

"We'll have to cross one at a time," I say, my voice barely above a whisper. "Riku, you take the rear. Make sure no one falls behind."

He nods, his jaw clenched tight. I turn to the women, their faces drawn and pale beneath the grime. "You'll need to be careful. Take it slow, and don't look down."

One by one, they step forward, their movements hesitant, their hands trembling as they grip the rough stone. I guide them across, my heart in my throat with each precarious step. The ravine seems to stretch on forever, a gaping maw waiting to swallow us whole.

Halfway across, one of the women stumbles, a cry of fear escaping her lips. I lunge forward, catching her arm just as she pitches towards the edge. For a moment, we teeter there, suspended between life and death, the weight of her unborn child pulling us down.

"I've got you," I breathe, my fingers digging into her flesh. "Just hold on."

Slowly, I ease her back onto the narrow path, my breath coming in ragged gasps. She clings to me, her body shaking with silent sobs. I murmur reassurances, hollow words that taste like ashes on my tongue.

We press on, each step a battle against the fear that claws at our throats. The weight of their lives hangs heavy on my shoulders, a burden I bear willingly, even as it threatens to crush me.

At last, we reach the other side, stumbling onto solid ground. I allow myself a moment to breathe, to let the relief wash over me in a dizzying wave. But it's short-lived, the knowledge of what lies ahead already gnawing at the edges of my mind.

"We keep moving," I say, my voice hoarse with exhaustion. "We don't stop until we find shelter."

Riku falls into step beside me, his presence a silent comfort. Together, we lead the way deeper into the shadows, the whispers of the dead trailing behind us like a macabre echo.

A piercing shriek shatters the eerie stillness, sending icy tendrils of dread down my spine. I whirl around, my heart pounding against my ribs, as a pack of feral undead bursts from the undergrowth, their twisted limbs flailing in a grotesque dance of hunger.

"Riku!" I shout, my voice raw with fear. "Protect the women!"

We spring into action, our weapons slicing through the fetid air. I lunge forward, my blade finding its mark in the rotting flesh of a snarling corpse. It crumples to the ground, only to be replaced by another, its eyes gleaming with an insatiable thirst for living flesh.

The survivors fight back, their cries of terror mingling with the sickening crunch of bones and the wet squelch of decaying flesh. Each swing of their weapons is fueled by a desperate, primal need to survive, to cling to the fragile thread of life that binds us all.

I lose myself in the rhythm of the battle, my mind numb to the horror that surrounds me. The world narrows to the space between each heartbeat, each ragged breath, each flash of my blade as it cleaves through the horde.

"Maikoru, behind you!" Riku's warning cuts through the chaos, and I spin around, my sword already in motion. It bites deep into the skull of an undead woman, her once-beautiful face now a twisted mask of hunger.

As she falls, I catch a glimpse of the pregnant women, their faces contorted in terror as they huddle together, their hands wrapped protectively around their swollen bellies. The sight of them, so vulnerable and afraid, sends a surge of rage coursing through my veins.

"I won't let them touch you," I growl, my voice low and fierce. "I swear it on my life."

I throw myself back into the fray, my blade singing a haunting melody of death. The undead press in from all sides, their numbers seemingly endless, but I refuse to yield. I fight with a fury born of desperation, each strike a silent prayer for the lives that hang in the balance.

The battle rages on, the forest floor slick with blood and gore. My muscles burn with exhaustion, my lungs screaming for air, but still, I fight. I fight for the women who carry the future within them, for the hope that flickers like a dying ember in the darkness.

And finally, as the last of the undead falls, I sink to my knees, my sword slipping from my grasp. I am dimly aware of Riku at my side, his hand on my shoulder, his voice a distant murmur. But all I can see are the faces of the survivors, their eyes wide with a fragile, tentative hope.

"We're alive," I whisper, my voice barely more than a rasp. "We made it."

But even as the words leave my lips, I know that this is only the beginning. The road ahead is long and treacherous, and the ghosts of our past will never stop haunting us. We are the walking wounded, the ones who have stared into the abyss and come back changed.

And yet, as I struggle to my feet, I feel a flicker of something that might almost be hope. It is a fragile thing, a gossamer thread that could snap at any moment, but it is enough. Enough to keep me moving forward, one step at a time, into the uncertain future that awaits us all.

The weight of the world bears down upon my shoulders, a burden I can never escape. As we press onward, the shadows of the rainforest close in around us, suffocating and oppressive. The silence is broken only by the distant moans of the undead, a constant reminder of the horrors that lurk just beyond the veil.

Riku walks beside me, his presence a small comfort in this endless nightmare. Our footsteps fall in perfect synchronicity, a testament to the bond we share. Born of blood and forged in the fires of this apocalypse, our friendship is the one thing that keeps me tethered to my humanity.

"Do you remember the promise we made, back when we were just kids?" Riku's voice is low, almost lost beneath the rustling of leaves.

I nod, a ghost of a smile tugging at my lips. "We said we'd always have each other's backs, no matter what."

"And we always will." Riku's hand finds mine, his grip strong and sure. "Until the end."

But even as he speaks the words, I feel a chill run down my spine. For in this world, the end is always just one misstep away. One moment of weakness, one wrong turn, and everything we've fought for could come crumbling down like a house of cards.

We continue on, the weight of our sins heavy upon our souls. The pregnant women walk behind us, their faces drawn and haggard. They are the reason we fight, the reason we cling to this fragile existence with every fiber of our being. For in their wombs lies the hope of a new beginning, a chance at redemption for all the wrongs we've done.

But as the shadows lengthen and the night draws near, I cannot shake the feeling that something is watching us from the depths of the rainforest. Something ancient and malevolent, biding its time until the moment is right to strike. And when it does, I fear that even Riku and I will not be enough to stop it.

For in this world of the dead, hope is a fragile thing indeed. And the ghosts of our past are always waiting, just beyond the edge of the firelight, ready to drag us down into the depths of our own personal hell.

The path ahead is treacherous, the air thick with the stench of decay. We move forward, our steps heavy with exhaustion, our hearts burdened by the weight of our sins. The pregnant women follow close behind, their breaths coming in short, ragged gasps. I can feel their fear, a palpable thing that hangs in the air like a shroud.

"Keep moving," I urge them, my voice barely above a whisper. "We're almost there."

But even as the words leave my lips, I know they are a lie. There is no sanctuary, no safe haven waiting for us at the end of this journey. There is only the next fight, the next desperate struggle for survival in a world gone mad.

Riku moves beside me, his eyes scanning the shadows for any sign of movement. I can see the tension in his jaw, the way his fingers twitch towards his weapon at the slightest sound. He knows, as I do, that death lurks around every corner, waiting to claim us at any moment.

And then, without warning, it is upon us. A lone figure staggers out from behind a tree, its flesh hanging in rotting strips from its bones. Its eyes are empty sockets, its mouth a gaping maw of blackened teeth. It lets out a moan, a sound that sends shivers down my spine.

"Riku!" I shout, my voice cracking with fear. "Take the left!"

He nods, his face set in grim determination as he charges forward, his blade flashing in the dim light. I move to the right, my own weapon at the ready. The creature lunges at me, its bony fingers grasping for my throat. I dodge, my heart pounding in my chest as I bring my blade down in a vicious arc.

The ghosts of my past dance around me, taunting me with visions of my failures and my sins. But I cannot let them win, not when so much is at stake. I fight on, my muscles screaming with the effort, my breath coming in short, ragged gasps.

And then, as quickly as it began, it is over. The creature lies still at my feet, its head severed from its body. I stand there, my chest heaving, my hands shaking with the aftermath of the battle.

"Is everyone alright?" I ask, my voice hoarse with exhaustion.

The pregnant women nod, their faces pale and drawn. Riku stands beside me, his blade dripping with black ichor. He looks at me, his eyes haunted by the same demons that torment my own soul.

"We have to keep moving," he says, his voice barely above a whisper. "They'll be more of them coming."

I nod, my heart heavy with the knowledge of what lies ahead. For in this world of the dead, there is no rest, no respite from the horrors that stalk our every step. We are the damned, the forsaken, doomed to wander this blighted earth until the end of our days.

But still, we press on, our steps heavy with the weight of our sins, our hearts burdened by the ghosts of our past. For in the end, what choice do we have? To lay down and die, to surrender to the darkness that threatens to consume us all?

No, we will fight on, even as the shadows lengthen and the night draws near. For in this world of the dead, hope is all we have left, a fragile flame flickering in the darkness, guiding us ever onwards towards an uncertain future.

I take a deep breath, the humid air filling my lungs as I survey the group before me. The pregnant women cradle their swollen bellies, their eyes wide with a mixture of fear and determination. Riku stands tall beside them, his blade at the ready, a silent guardian against the horrors that lurk in the shadows.

"We keep moving," I say, my voice a low growl. "We don't stop until we reach the sanctuary."

The group nods, their faces grim with resolve. We set off once more, pushing through the dense foliage, our steps muffled by the thick carpet of leaves beneath our feet. The rainforest seems to close in around us, the trees pressing in on all sides, their branches reaching out like grasping fingers.

But we press on, driven by the desperate hope that somewhere out there, beyond the endless sea of green, lies a place of safety, a haven from the nightmare that has consumed our world.

As we walk, my mind wanders to the past, to the sins that haunt my every waking moment. I see the faces of those I failed to save, their eyes accusing in the darkness. I feel the weight of my failures pressing down upon me, threatening to crush me beneath their burden.

But I push those thoughts aside, focusing instead on the task at hand. For in this world, there is no room for regret, no time for mourning. There is only the fight, the desperate struggle to survive in the face of overwhelming odds.

We move deeper into the rainforest, the air growing thicker, more oppressive with each passing step. The sounds of the jungle fade away, replaced by an eerie silence that sends a chill down my spine.

And then, in the distance, I hear it - the low, mournful wail of the undead, carried on the wind like a portent of doom. My blood runs cold at the sound, my grip tightening on the hilt of my sword.

Besides me, Riku tenses, his eyes scanning the shadows for any sign of movement. "They're coming," he whispers, his voice barely audible over the pounding of my own heart.

I nod, my jaw clenched tight with grim determination. "Then let them come," I say, my voice a low growl. "We'll be ready for them."

And with that, we press on, our steps quickening as we race towards our elusive sanctuary, the weight of our sins and the ghosts of our past spurring us ever onwards into the waiting arms of fate.

As we forge ahead through the dense undergrowth, the shadows seem to lengthen and twist, taking on a life of their own. The air grows thick and heavy, pressing down upon us like a physical weight. Each breath is a struggle, as if the very atmosphere is conspiring to suffocate us.

Riku, ever the keen observer, suddenly stops in his tracks. His eyes narrow as he scans the surrounding foliage, his body tense and coiled like a spring. "Wait," he hisses, his voice low and urgent. "There's something up ahead."

I follow his gaze, my own senses straining to penetrate the gloom. At first, I see nothing but the endless sea of green, the trees and vines blending together in a dizzying tapestry. But then, as my eyes adjust to the dim light, I catch a glimpse of something hidden in the shadows - a narrow path, barely visible amidst the dense undergrowth.

"A trail," I murmur, my heart quickening with a sudden surge of hope. "Could it lead to shelter?"

Riku nods, his expression grim. "Only one way to find out."

Together, we push forward, our steps cautious and measured as we navigate the treacherous terrain. The path winds and twists like a serpent, leading us deeper into the heart of the rainforest. With each passing moment, the sense of unease grows stronger, the feeling that we are being watched by unseen eyes.

Just as the tension becomes almost unbearable, we emerge into a small clearing. And there, before us, is a sight that takes our breath away - a hidden waterfall, its crystal-clear waters cascading down from a rocky cliff face into a tranquil pool below.

"Water," Riku breathes, his voice thick with relief. "We can rest here, refill our supplies."

I nod, my own throat suddenly parched with thirst. We make our way to the water's edge, our movements sluggish with exhaustion. As we kneel down to drink, the cool liquid soothing our cracked lips and dry throats, I can't shake the feeling that this moment of respite is only temporary.

For in this world, peace is fleeting, and danger lurks around every corner. And even as we take this brief moment to rest and gather our strength, I know that the road ahead will only grow darker and more perilous with each passing day.

With our water supplies replenished and our spirits lifted, if only for a moment, we gather our belongings and prepare to continue our journey. The pregnant women move with a newfound determination, their hands resting protectively on their swollen bellies as they navigate the uneven ground.

Riku falls into step beside me, his eyes scanning the surrounding foliage for any signs of danger. "We can't stay here long," he murmurs, his voice low and urgent. "The undead are never far behind."

I nod, my grip tightening on my weapon. "We keep moving," I reply, my voice steady despite the fear that gnaws at my insides. "We don't stop until we reach the safe haven."

As we set off once more, the sound of the waterfall fading into the distance behind us, I can't help but feel a flicker of hope stirring in my chest. It's a fragile thing, easily extinguished by the harsh realities of this world, but it's there nonetheless.

For in the midst of all this darkness and despair, there is still a glimmer of light to be found. It's in the determined faces of the survivors who follow me, in the unbreakable bond I share with Riku, and in the life that grows within the pregnant women who walk beside us.

And it's this light, however faint, that propels us forward, even as the shadows close in around us and the cries of the undead echo in the distance. We know that the path ahead is treacherous, that there will be more battles to fight and more losses to endure.

But we also know that we are not alone in this struggle. We have each other, and we have the hope that someday, somehow, we will find the safe haven we so desperately seek.

So we press on, our steps fueled by a renewed sense of purpose and determination. The rainforest may be dark and menacing, the undead may be relentless in their pursuit, but we will not falter.

For we are survivors, and we will not rest until we have found the sanctuary we so richly deserve.

The oppressive heat of the rainforest pressed in around me as I stepped into the clearing, feeble shafts of light streaming through the thick canopy. My ragged band of survivors emerged from the foliage behind me, their grimy faces etched with weariness and the hungry look of those who'd seen too much death. Osamu stood at the center, a weathered silhouette against the verdant backdrop. Something about his grim stance sent a shiver down my spine, despite the cloying humidity.

"You've come to learn the ways of survival," Osamu said, his voice low and gravelly like ancient stones rubbing together. "In this godforsaken world of the undead, only those who master stealth and precision will live to see another day."

He reached behind him, producing a long wooden spear. With fluid movements belying his age, he twirled the weapon in a mesmerizing arc. My eyes followed the polished tip as it glinted in the weak light.

Osamu lunged forward, thrusting the spear at an imagined foe. His arm snapped like a whip, the deadly point blurring with speed. In my mind's eye, I could see it piercing a zombie's skull, erupting in a geyser of fetid gore. The thought both thrilled and sickened me.

Next, he unslung a blowgun from his back - a long, slender tube of hollowed bamboo. Osamu loaded a dart, raising it to his withered lips. His cheeks ballooned as he took aim at an unseen target. With a sharp exhalation, the dart flew true, disappearing into the gloom. A lethal whisper.

I glanced at the others, seeing the unease on their faces. Kimiko, ever stoic, watched Osamu with hard eyes. Takashi's lip curled with disgust, no doubt imagining the rotted flesh of the undead. Hana trembled, clutching her swollen belly. I felt the weight of my past sins press upon me, the lives I'd failed to save. Their ghostly fingers clawed at my soul.

In this nightmarish world, we all bore the scars of survival. The things we'd done...the horrors we'd witnessed...they haunted us, even in the light of day. And now, as we gathered to learn the arts of death from an old man cloaked in shadow, I couldn't help but wonder:

In the end, would we become the very monsters we sought to destroy?

Maikoru and the others practice their weapon handling, focusing on their aim and accuracy. They aim for targets set up in the clearing, honing their skills and adjusting their techniques as needed:

I gripped the spear, its weight familiar yet alien in my hands. The rough-hewn wood seemed to pulse with a life of its own, a conduit for the primal energies that surged through my veins. Around me, the others readied their own weapons - blowguns, bows, and crude clubs fashioned from jungle hardwood.

Across the clearing, a line of makeshift targets stood in mute challenge. Woven mats of palm fronds, each adorned with a crudely drawn human face. No, not human. The faces were gaunt and twisted, with hollow eyes and gaping mouths. The faces of the undead.

Osamu's voice rang out, sharp and commanding. "Begin!"

I drew back my arm, feeling the coiled power in my muscles. The spear balanced on my fingertips, poised like a viper ready to strike. I fixed my gaze on the nearest target, imagining it as a shambling corpse, its rotted visage leering at me. With a grunt, I hurled the spear, watching it arc through the air.

It struck the target dead center, the point sinking deep into the woven mat. A kill shot. Beside me, Kimiko loosed an arrow from her bow, the shaft burying itself in another target's eye socket. Takashi's club smashed into a third, obliterating the dummy's head in a spray of splinters.

We worked in grim silence, the only sounds the thunk of weapons striking targets and the rasp of our breath. Sweat poured down my face, stinging my eyes. My arms ached with the strain of hurling spear after spear, but I embraced the pain, relished it. Each target became a repository for my rage, my sorrow, my guilt. I imagined the faces of those I'd lost - my wife, my children, my friends. I saw them as they had been in life, and as they must have been in death, ravaged by the undead plague.

And I killed them, over and over again.

Osamu leads the group on a stealth exercise, teaching them how to move silently through the dense undergrowth without alerting the undead or other potential threats:

The jungle closed around us like a living thing, a green hell of tangled vines and grasping thorns. Osamu moved through it like a wraith, his steps silent, his passage unmarked. We followed, struggling to emulate his ghost-like grace.

"The undead have no sight, no hearing," Osamu whispered, his voice barely audible above the drone of insects. "They hunt by scent, by the heat of living flesh. To move undetected, you must become one with the jungle. You must be as cold and silent as the dead themselves."

I felt the weight of his words, the bitter truth of them. To survive in this world, we had to embrace the qualities of the very things we feared. We had to become like them.

Step by step, we wound our way through the undergrowth, placing our feet with exacting care. The crunch of a leaf, the snap of a twig - any sound could betray our presence to the lurking horrors. Sweat soaked my shirt, plastering it to my skin. Insects crawled across my face, my arms, my legs, but I dared not brush them away. To move was to die.

Time lost all meaning in that green gloom. Minutes stretched into hours, hours into lifetimes. The jungle watched us with a thousand unseen eyes, waiting for us to falter, to make that one fatal mistake.

But we endured, driven by the implacable will to survive. And when at last we reached the far side of the undergrowth, emerging into the blessed light of day, I felt a grim sense of triumph. We had passed through the valley of the shadow, and come out the other side.

But even as I savored this small victory, I knew it was only the beginning. The real test was yet to come, when we faced not the passive menace of the jungle, but the active hunger of the undead. On that day, we would learn the true measure of our skills, and the depths of our resolve.

We would learn what it meant to be survivors in a world gone mad.

The vines felt rough and unyielding in my hands as I wove them into a deadly snare. Nearby, the others worked with grim determination, their faces etched with concentration. We were learning the art of trapping, the subtle science of using the jungle's own bounty against our enemies.

Osamu moved among us, his weathered hands guiding our clumsy efforts. "Like this," he said, his voice a low murmur. "The knots must be tight, the trigger well-hidden. One mistake, and your trap becomes useless."

I nodded, my fingers aching as I pulled the vines taut. It was tedious work, but I understood its importance. In this war, every advantage counted. A single well-placed trap could mean the difference between life and death.

As we labored, my mind wandered to darker places. I thought of the undead, those shambling horrors that had once been human. What did they feel, as they stumbled through the jungle in their mindless pursuit of flesh? Did some part of them still remember their past lives, or were they nothing more than empty shells, driven by an insatiable hunger?

Osamu's voice snapped me back to the present. "The head," he said, tapping his temple for emphasis. "That is the weakness of the undead. Destroy the brain, and you destroy the monster."

He picked up a sharpened stake, its tip gleaming in the dappled sunlight. With a swift, sure motion, he drove it into the trunk of a nearby tree. The wood splintered under the force of the blow, and I flinched involuntarily.

"You must strike hard and true," Osamu continued, his eyes burning with a fierce intensity. "Hesitate, and you are lost. The undead do not feel pain, do not know fear. They will keep coming until they are destroyed utterly."

I swallowed hard, my mouth suddenly dry. The thought of facing those creatures in close combat, of driving a stake through their skulls, filled me with a sickening dread. But I knew I had no choice. If I wanted to survive, I would have to become a killer.

And so I practiced, striking at the tree again and again until my arms trembled with fatigue. The wood splintered and cracked under my blows, but I barely noticed. All that mattered was the rhythm of the strikes, the feel of the stake in my hand.

In that moment, I felt something shift inside me. A hardness, a cold determination that I had never known before. I was no longer the man I had once been - the soft, civilized creature of the old world. I was something new, something forged in the crucible of this merciless jungle.

I was a survivor. And I would do whatever it took to stay that way.

As the sun began to dip towards the horizon, Osamu called us together once more. "You have learned to fight," he said, his voice low and serious. "But to truly survive, you must also learn to hide."

He led us deeper into the jungle, to a small clearing where the trees grew thick and close. There, he showed us how to gather mud and leaves, how to smear them over our skin and clothing until we blended seamlessly with the shadows.

I watched as the others disappeared into the undergrowth, their forms melting away like ghosts. Only the gleam of their eyes remained, glinting in the fading light.

"To be unseen is to be safe," Osamu whispered, his voice seeming to come from everywhere and nowhere at once. "The undead hunt by sight and sound. If they cannot find you, they cannot kill you."

I nodded, my heart pounding in my chest. The thought of being so vulnerable, so exposed, sent a thrill of fear through me. But at the same time, I felt a strange exhilaration. To be one with the jungle, to move like a shadow among the trees - it was a kind of power I had never known.

And so I practiced, slipping silently through the undergrowth, my senses straining for any sign of danger. The mud felt cool and slick against my skin, the leaves rustling softly as I passed.

At times, I caught glimpses of the others - a flash of movement in the corner of my eye, a muffled footfall that could have been nothing more than the wind. But for the most part, we were alone, each of us lost in our own silent world.

As the darkness deepened around us, I felt a growing sense of unease. The jungle seemed to come alive at night, filled with strange sounds and shadowy forms that lurked just beyond the edge of sight.

But I pushed down my fear, focusing instead on the task at hand. I would not let the darkness defeat me. I would learn to master it, to bend it to my will.

For in this world of blood and death, only the strong could hope to survive. And I was determined to be one of them.

The mock battles were a brutal awakening, a stark reminder of the horrors we would soon face. Osamu had us pair off, each taking turns as the undead aggressors, our movements slow and jerky, our eyes vacant and hungry.

I faced off against Takeshi, a young man with a quick wit and a quicker blade. He lunged at me, his movements precise and deadly, and I barely managed to dodge the blow. I could feel the rush of air as his makeshift spear whistled past my face, close enough to make my heart skip a beat.

"Too slow, Maikoru," he taunted, a wicked grin spreading across his face. "The undead won't give you a second chance."

I gritted my teeth and launched myself at him, my own spear held low and ready. We danced around each other, striking and parrying, our breaths coming in ragged gasps as we pushed ourselves to the limit.

I have to be faster, I thought, my mind racing as I searched for an opening. *I have to be smarter, more agile. I have to...*

And then it happened. Takeshi's foot caught on a root, and he stumbled, his balance thrown off for just a moment. I seized the opportunity, driving my spear forward with all my strength.

The blow struck home, the sharpened point sinking deep into Takeshi's chest. He let out a strangled cry and fell to the ground, his body twitching and convulsing as the life drained from him.

I stood over him, my chest heaving, my heart pounding in my ears. *I did it,* I thought, a sense of grim satisfaction washing over me. *I beat him.*

But even as the thought formed in my mind, I felt a creeping sense of unease. *This is just a game,* I reminded myself, my eyes fixed on Takeshi's still form. *When the real battles come, will I be ready?*

I had little time to dwell on such thoughts, for Osamu was already calling us to the next challenge. The obstacle course loomed before us, a twisting maze of fallen logs, tangled vines, and hidden traps.

"Your agility and wits will be put to the test," Osamu declared, his voice ringing out through the clearing. "You must navigate the course as quickly as possible, while avoiding the dangers that lurk within."

I swallowed hard, my mouth suddenly dry. I had always prided myself on my physical prowess, but this was a different kind of challenge altogether.

As I stepped up to the starting line, I could feel the eyes of the others on me, watching, judging. *I cannot fail,* I thought, my jaw clenched tight. *I will not fail.*

And then Osamu gave the signal, and I was off, sprinting into the maze with reckless abandon. The world narrowed to a single point of focus, my breath coming in sharp, ragged gasps as I vaulted over fallen trees and ducked beneath low-hanging vines.

Faster, I urged myself, my legs pumping furiously. *Faster, faster, faster...*

But even as I pushed myself to the limit, I could feel the traps closing in around me. A trip wire here, a hidden pit there - each one a deadly reminder of the risks we faced.

I leaped over a fallen log, my heart in my throat as I sailed through the air. For a moment, I thought I had made it - but then my foot caught on something, and I was falling, tumbling head over heels into the undergrowth.

I landed hard, the breath knocked from my lungs. *I failed,* was all I could think as I lay there, gasping for air. *I failed, and now they will all see me for the weakling I am.*

But even as the thought formed in my mind, I heard Osamu's voice, cutting through the haze of pain and shame.

"Get up, Maikoru," he said, his tone brooking no argument. "The undead do not rest, and neither can we."

I struggled to my feet, my body aching, my pride bruised. But as I looked around at the others, their faces set with grim determination, I knew that I could not give up.

I will learn, I vowed, my fists clenched at my sides. *I will adapt, and I will survive. No matter what it takes.*

The night wrapped around us like a suffocating shroud as we ventured into the heart of darkness. Osamu's voice, a haunting whisper, guided us through the inky void. "Your eyes deceive you," he warned. "Trust your other senses, for they will be your salvation."

I closed my eyes, allowing the shadows to envelop me. The rustling of leaves, the snapping of twigs underfoot - every sound amplified, a symphony of dread. The stench of decay, the coppery tang of blood - the undead were near, their presence a palpable force.

Focus, I told myself, my breath shallow and ragged. *You've trained for this. You can do this.*

We moved as one, a silent unit, our weapons at the ready. The darkness pressed in around us, alive with unseen threats. I could feel their eyes upon me, the undead, watching, waiting for the perfect moment to strike.

A twig snapped behind me, and I whirled around, my spear thrust outward. But there was nothing there, only the mocking laughter of the night.

You're losing it, a voice whispered in my head. *You're going to get everyone killed.*

I shook my head, trying to banish the doubts that plagued me. *I can't think like that,* I told myself. *I have to stay focused, stay sharp.*

And then, without warning, they were upon us.

The undead surged forward, a wave of rotting flesh and gnashing teeth. We met them head-on, our weapons flashing in the moonlight. I thrust my spear into the eye socket of a shambling corpse, the bones crunching sickeningly as the creature fell.

But there were too many of them, an endless tide of horror. I could hear the screams of my fellow tribesmen, the wet, tearing sounds of flesh being rent from bone.

This is it, I thought, a strange calm settling over me. *This is how I die.*

But even as the thought formed in my mind, I felt a hand grasp my shoulder. It was Osamu, his face a mask of determination. "Stand firm, Maikoru," he said, his voice cutting through the chaos. "We fight as one."

Together, we pushed back against the horde, our movements fluid and precise. We danced a deadly waltz, our weapons singing a song of death. The undead fell before us, their bodies piling up in grotesque heaps.

And then, as suddenly as it had begun, it was over. The clearing was silent, save for the ragged breathing of the survivors. I looked around, my eyes wide with disbelief.

We did it, I thought, a surge of pride welling up within me. *We actually did it.*

But even as the thought formed in my mind, I saw Osamu shake his head. "This was only a test," he said, his voice grave. "The true horrors still await us."

I swallowed hard, my mouth suddenly dry. *He's right,* I realized, a chill running down my spine. *This is only the beginning.*

The final test was over, but the real battle had yet to begin. The weight of responsibility settled heavily upon my shoulders as I looked out into the darkness, knowing that the fate of our people rested in our hands.

We will fight, I vowed, my grip tightening on my spear. *We will survive. No matter the cost.*

As the adrenaline faded, I felt a wave of exhaustion wash over me. My muscles ached, and my mind was weary from the constant vigilance. I looked around at my fellow tribesmen, seeing the same fatigue etched upon their faces.

Yet beneath the weariness, I saw something else: a glimmer of hope, a spark of determination. We had faced the horrors of the night and emerged victorious. We had proven to ourselves that we were capable of more than we ever thought possible.

Osamu stepped forward, his eyes scanning the group. "You have done well," he said, his voice filled with quiet pride. "But do not let this victory blind you to the challenges that lie ahead."

He paused, his gaze distant as if seeing beyond the present moment. "The world has changed, and we must change with it. We must adapt, or we will perish."

I nodded, knowing the truth of his words. The undead were not the only threat we faced. There were other dangers lurking in the shadows, waiting to strike when we least expected it.

"We must stay vigilant," Osamu continued, his voice growing more urgent. "We must trust in each other, for our strength lies in our unity. Alone, we are vulnerable, but together, we are unstoppable."

I felt a surge of emotion rising within me, a fierce determination to protect my people at all costs. I looked around at the faces of my fellow tribesmen, seeing the same resolve mirrored in their eyes.

We are one, I thought, my heart swelling with pride. *We are the last hope for our people, and we will not fail them.*

Osamu's voice broke through my thoughts, his words a solemn reminder of the road ahead. "Remember what you have learned here," he said, his gaze sweeping over the group. "Remember the skills you have honed, the bonds you have forged. For they will be your greatest weapons in the battles to come."

I took a deep breath, letting his words sink in. We had come so far, but there was still so much further to go. The path ahead was shrouded in darkness, but I knew that we would face it together, united by our common purpose.

We are the survivors, I thought, my grip tightening on my spear. *And we will fight until our last breath.*

As the sun began to set over the rainforest, casting long shadows across the clearing, we dispersed, each of us seeking a moment of solitude to prepare for the trials ahead. I found myself drawn to the edge of the clearing, where the trees grew tall and dense, their leaves rustling in the gentle breeze.

I leaned against the rough bark of a towering tree, closing my eyes and inhaling deeply. The scent of the rainforest filled my nostrils, a heady mix of earth and decay, of life and death. It was a reminder of the constant cycle of existence, of the endless struggle between the living and the undead.

How long can we keep fighting? I wondered, my thoughts turning dark. *How long before we succumb to the same fate as the rest of the world?*

But even as the doubts crept in, I felt a flicker of hope, a stubborn refusal to give in to despair. We had come too far to surrender now, had sacrificed too much to let the undead claim victory.

I opened my eyes, scanning the faces of my fellow tribesmen. They were a ragtag group, battered and bruised, but there was a fierce determination in their eyes, a willingness to fight until their last breath.

We are the last of the living, I thought, my resolve hardening. *And we will not go quietly into the night.*

I pushed myself away from the tree, my muscles coiled with tension. The battles ahead would be brutal, the odds stacked against us, but we had no choice but to face them head-on.

For our people, I thought, my hand tightening around the hilt of my knife. *For our future.*

As the last rays of sunlight faded from the sky, I turned to face my fellow survivors, my voice low and steady.

"It's time," I said, my words heavy with the weight of what was to come. "Let's move out."

And with that, we stepped forward into the darkness, ready to face the horrors that awaited us, united by our shared purpose and unbreakable bond.

The moans of the dead shattered the still night air. They came without warning, an undulating mass of rotting flesh emerging from the shadows.

"Zombies!" someone screamed. The camp erupted into chaos. Shouts of terror mixed with inhuman snarls as the horde descended upon us.

I leapt to my feet, heart hammering in my chest. Beside me, Riku was already in motion, barking orders. "Form a defensive line! Grab your weapons!"

His authoritative voice cut through the panic, spurring the survivors to action. They scrambled for guns, blades, anything to hold back the tide of undead.

I hefted my crossbow, the weight familiar and grounding amidst the madness. How had they found us? Was nowhere safe? The questions rattled in my skull.

"Maikoru! Left flank!" Riku called, machete glinting in his hand. I nodded curtly and raced to my position, directing the others into formation as I went. We made a ragged line, a flimsy barrier against the sea of grasping hands and snapping jaws.

"Hold steady!" I shouted over the din. "Aim for the head!" A bitter, humorless laugh escaped my lips. As if they needed reminding after all this time. After all we'd lost.

The first wave hit, and the night dissolved into blood and bullets, the air rent by screams both living and dead. We fought like cornered animals, desperate and savage. Because that's what we were now, stripped of our humanity by this merciless apocalypse.

I loosed arrow after arrow into the fray, each one finding its mark with a sickening thud. Beside me, the others fought with a ferocity born of despair, hackinng and slashing. But still the horde pressed forward, an inexorable wall of death.

"There's too many!" a woman screamed, voice cracking in desperation. "We can't hold them!"

Deep down, a traitorous voice whispered that she was right. That this was the end. That all our struggles had been for nothing.

I shook my head savagely, denying the insidious doubts. No. We would not fall here. I would not let these soulless monsters claim anyone else. Especially not him.

My eyes met Riku's across the battle. In that glance, I saw my own fearddesperation mirrored. Along with a grim, unyielding determination. We would live. We had to.

Together, we rallied the survivors for one last stand against the ravenous dead. I prayed it would be enough.

The stench of rot and gunpowder choked the air as we fought like the damned, knowing that's exactly what we'd become if we faltered. Riku and I moved as one, blades and arrows singing a deadly duet. He covered my back while I picked off the more distant threats, an unspoken rhythm honed by countless battles.

"Maikoru, on your left!" Riku's warning sliced through the cacophony.

I pivoted, heart lurching as a zombie lunged for me, its putrid jaws snapping inches from my face. Gritting my teeth, I jammed an arrow through its eye socket, gore splattering my skin as it crumpled.

"Too close," I panted, hands trembling minutely as I nocked another arrow. "Getting sloppy in my old age."

Riku barked a strained laugh, machete cleaving through decaying flesh. "Never. The day you get sloppy is the day I hang up my blade."

A gurgling snarl wrenched our focus back to the battle, the brief levity snuffed out. We danced a macabre waltz with death, every breath a fleeting victory. The others fought with equal parts terror and tenacity, the same desperate litany echoing in all our minds:

Live. Please, God, just let us live.

Time lost meaning in the crimson-soaked chaos. Minutes bled into hours, exhaustion seeping into every swing and shot. But somehow, against all odds, the tide began to turn.

"Push them back!" Riku roared. "We're going to beat these rotten bastards!"

His words kindled a last, desperate surge of hope. I clung to it like a drowning man, letting it fuel limbs that wanted to buckle. We would live. We had to.

Because the alternative was one I refused to contemplate. Not after everything we'd endured. Not when we'd already lost so much.

[I'll stop here to allow you to direct the scene further or provide feedback. Just let me know how you'd like me to proceed!]

The momentary elation shattered as a piercing scream cut through the fray. My head snapped towards the sound, heart plummeting at the sight that greeted me.

Taro, sweet, gentle Taro, disappeared beneath a swarm of grasping hands and gnashing teeth. His cries dissolved into wet, rattling gurgles, the undead tearing into him with savage frenzy.

I froze, bile scorching my throat. He was just a boy, barely seventeen. He didn't deserve this. None of us did.

Riku's anguished bellow jolted me back to reality. He lunged towards Taro, hacking frantically at the zombies, but it was too late. The light had already faded from those once-bright eyes, leaving only glassy emptiness.

Despair threatened to engulf me, a yawning chasm of grief and futility. How could we possibly hope to survive this? What was the point of fighting, when death claimed us so easily?

But as I watched Riku, saw the raw, unrelenting fury etched into every line of his blood-splattered face, something within me hardened. No. I refused to succumb. For Taro, for everyone we'd lost, we had to keep going. We owed them that much.

I drew back my bow with a snarl, letting the rage and sorrow fuel me. The arrow found its mark, then another, and another, each one a silent promise. Beside me, Riku moved like a man possessed, his machete an extension of his will, an instrument of retribution.

We fought with renewed savagery, our movements mechanical, devoid of thought or feeling. There was only the next target, the next kill, the next heartbeat. Survive. Protect. Endure.

The world narrowed to blood and steel, the stench of death thick in my nostrils. I didn't feel the ache in my muscles, the sting of wounds I didn't remember receiving. All that mattered was the battle, the desperate need to keep my people alive.

Because if we fell, if we let the darkness claim us, then Taro's death would be meaningless. And that was a failure I couldn't bear.

So I fought, and kept fighting, even as the horde pressed closer, even as the weight of our losses threatened to crush me. I would not let them take anyone else. Not today. Not while I still drew breath.

The tide turned, slowly but surely. Our relentless assault thinned the horde, and I saw a flicker of hope in the eyes of the survivors. They fought with renewed vigor, their exhaustion giving way to grim determination.

"Keep pushing!" I shouted, my voice hoarse. "We're almost through!"

Riku grunted in acknowledgment, his machete cleaving through a zombie's skull. We were so close, so damn close to victory I could taste it.

But fate, it seemed, had a twisted sense of humor.

A hulking figure burst through the defensive line, a grotesque parody of a man. Its bloated flesh hung in tatters, revealing the glistening muscle and bone beneath. Its eyes, milky white and bulging, fixed on me with a hunger that chilled my soul.

The survivors faltered, their momentary hope replaced by a primal terror. I couldn't blame them. This zombie was different, a nightmarish aberration that defied explanation.

It lumbered forward, its movements jerky and unnatural, yet possessed of a horrible strength. I saw the fear in Riku's eyes, a fear I knew was mirrored in my own.

"Maikoru..." he whispered, his voice trembling.

I swallowed hard, my grip tightening on my bow. "We hold the line," I said, my words a fragile mask for the dread that gripped me. "No matter what."

The creature roared, a sound that seemed to shake the very earth beneath our feet. It charged, its massive form barreling towards us with a speed that belied its size.

I loosed an arrow, then another, but they seemed to have no effect. The beast kept coming, its gaze locked on me, its maw gaping wide in a silent scream.

Riku stepped forward, his machete raised in defiance. "Together," he said, his voice steady despite the fear that danced in his eyes.

I nodded, drawing my knife. "Together."

We braced ourselves, two fragile humans against a nightmare made flesh. The creature bore down on us, its fetid breath washing over us like a wave of decay.

And as it closed the distance, as its massive hands reached for us, I couldn't help but wonder if this was the end. If, after all we'd endured, all we'd sacrificed, our journey would meet its conclusion here, in the grasp of this abomination.

But one thought rose above the fear, above the despair that threatened to consume me. One truth that had carried me through the darkest of times.

We were survivors. And we would not go quietly into the night.

With a cry of defiance, I lunged forward, my knife seeking the creature's flesh. Beside me, Riku did the same, his machete flashing in the fading light.

The zombie was strong, far stronger than any we'd faced before. It shrugged off our blows as if they were nothing, its rotting flesh absorbing the impact without so much as a flinch.

But we were relentless. We darted in and out, striking and retreating, a deadly dance of desperation and determination. The creature's arms swung wildly, its grasping hands missing us by mere inches as we wove around it.

Pain exploded in my shoulder as one of its blows found its mark, sending me stumbling back. I gritted my teeth, pushing the agony aside. There was no room for weakness, not now.

Riku, too, was flagging, his movements growing slower, more labored. Blood seeped from a gash on his forehead, mingling with the sweat that poured down his face.

But in his eyes, I saw the same resolve that burned in my own. The knowledge that we were all that stood between this monster and those we'd sworn to protect.

"We can't... let it win," Riku panted, his voice ragged with exhaustion.

I nodded, my grip tightening on my knife. "We won't."

And so we fought on, our bodies screaming in protest, our minds numb with fatigue. Time lost all meaning, the world narrowing to this one moment, this one battle.

The creature's blows grew more frenzied, more desperate, as if it sensed its own impending doom. But we were unrelenting, our weapons finding their mark again and again, tearing into putrid flesh and brittle bone.

Until, at last, with a final, shuddering groan, the zombie fell, its massive form crashing to the ground in a cloud of dust and decay.

We stood over it, chests heaving, bodies trembling with exhaustion and spent adrenaline. The silence that followed was deafening, broken only by our ragged breaths and the distant moans of the remaining undead.

But as I looked to Riku, saw the grim triumph in his eyes, I felt a flicker of something...

"Hold it off! I'll flank from the right!" Riku yelled over the guttural moans of the undead monstrosity. I nodded grimly, my eyes locked on the hulking zombie as it lumbered toward us with preternatural speed and viciousness. Its flesh hung in ragged strips, exposing yellowed bone and pulsating organs. Black blood oozed from countless wounds, a testament to the futility of our struggle. But still, we had to try. For the others. For redemption we didn't deserve.

I loosed arrow after arrow at the creature's misshapen skull as Riku darted to the side, his machete glinting crimson. The zombie swiped at him with gnarled claws but Riku rolled beneath the blow, slashing at hamstrings and knee tendons. Foul ichor sprayed his face. I felt a flicker of hope - maybe, just maybe we could bring it down.

That hope died as the zombie's arm bashed into my chest, sending me crashing to the blood-soaked earth. Pain lanced through my surely broken ribs. I coughed, tasting copper. Wheezing, I scrambled for my dropped bow, cursing my damnable luck, my wretched existence. Was this finally the end? Just as I reached for a final arrow, Riku's scream pierced the air.

"No!" I cried hoarsely, looking up to see the creature lifting Riku by the throat, his legs flailing. His machete tumbled from limp fingers. I had to do something. This fight was draining me of everything, but I couldn't let Riku fall. Not like the others...

Somehow, I staggered to my feet, nocking the arrow with trembling hands. Black spots swam in my vision. Riku gargled and writhed in the monster's grip. I drew back the bowstring, muscles quivering, focusing my last ounce of hate at the zombie's decaying eye socket.

"Let him go, you worm-ridden corpse," I snarled through gritted teeth, and released.

The arrow flew true, burying itself deep in the zombie's skull with a sickening crunch. It staggered, dropping Riku, who crumpled to the ground gasping for air. But still, the creature advanced, pulling itself along on shattered limbs, its one remaining eye fixed on me with soulless hunger.

I backed away, reaching for another arrow, but my quiver was empty. Despair clawed at my mind. So this was how it would end - devoured by this abomination, just another meaningless death in a world gone mad.

Suddenly, Riku surged forward with a roar, snatching up his machete. He leaped onto the zombie's back and hacked at its neck with frenzied swings, his face a rictus of fury and anguish.

"Die, you bastard!" he howled. "Die!"

With a final, wrenching slice, the creature's head tumbled free. The body collapsed, twitching, as Riku stood atop it, chest heaving, clothes drenched in gore. He met my gaze, and in that moment, I saw my own pain reflected back at me - the scars that would never heal, the void left by those we couldn't save.

Around us, the survivors emerged from the shadows, clutching improvised weapons, faces etched with shock and grief. They gathered their fallen friends, voices cracking with barely restrained sobs. The air hung heavy with the stench of death and smoke.

I limped to Riku's side, clasping his shoulder. "We did it," I rasped. "But the cost..." I couldn't finish, my throat constricting.

He nodded, eyes glistening. "We can't let their deaths be in vain. We have to keep going, keep fighting. For them."

I surveyed our ragged band, these desperate souls who looked to us for hope when we had none ourselves. My sins, my failures, they were chains I could never escape. But perhaps, in keeping the others alive, I could find some shred of redemption.

If the cruel fates allowed it.

Night fell like a shroud, smothering the last embers of our meager fire. In the stillness, the weight of leadership settled upon my shoulders, a burden I had never asked for but could not relinquish. Beside me, Riku sat in silence, his gaze distant, haunted by the ghosts of those we'd lost.

"Do you think we'll ever find a safe place?" he murmured, his voice barely audible above the chirping of crickets. "A home?"

I wanted to offer reassurance, to spin a tale of hope and redemption, but the words turned to ash on my tongue. "I don't know," I admitted, my honesty as bleak as the moonless sky. "But we have to keep trying. For their sake."

Riku nodded, his jaw clenched with determination. "We'll make them proud, Maikoru. We'll survive, no matter what it takes."

I wished I could share his conviction, but the specter of my past loomed large, a constant reminder of my failings. How long before my sins caught up with me, before the blood on my hands stained everything I touched?

As if sensing my thoughts, Riku placed a hand on my arm, his grip firm and grounding. "We're in this together," he said, his eyes boring into mine. "You're not alone."

I swallowed past the lump in my throat, grateful for his unwavering support. Together, we'd faced the horrors of this new world, and together, we'd continue to fight.

But even as I clung to that glimmer of solidarity, a chill crept down my spine, a whisper of foreboding that I couldn't shake. The road ahead stretched long and treacherous, a gauntlet of untold dangers and heartache. In the depths of my being, I knew that our trials were far from over.

For in this savage land, where the dead walked and the living trembled, there could be no peace, no respite. Only the unrelenting march of survival, one blood-soaked step at a time.

The undergrowth grabbed at my legs as I forced my way through the dense rainforest, each step a struggle against exhaustion and dread. Vines and foliage muffled our movements, but even so, I kept my grip tight on my machete, knuckles white, eyes scanning the shadows for movement. Had to stay vigilant. Had to protect them.

"Maikoru, wait up," Riku called softly from behind me. "The others are falling behind."

I paused, glancing back at the ragged group trudging in my wake. Their faces were gaunt, haunted. The same weariness that dragged at my own limbs reflected in their hopeless eyes.

"We can't afford to slow down," I said, trying to inject some authority into my voice. "Every second we linger, they get closer."

Yet even as I said it, doubt gnawed at my mind. Were we only delaying the inevitable? Leading them on a futile march to a salvation that didn't exist? The blood of those we'd lost already stained my hands. Their ghosts followed me through this godforsaken jungle.

I rubbed a hand over my face. "Five minutes. Then we move on."

Slumping down against a tree trunk, I let my eyes drift shut, but the images came unbidden. The people I've failed. The choices I've made. Were they tainted by the darkness within me? How much of the blood could I blame on cruel necessity—and how much on the twisted thing growing inside?

Through the thick canopy, the sun beat down, hot and oppressive. The rainforest loomed, watching, always watching with a thousand unseen eyes. I had to get them through this green hell. Had to cling to the fraying hope that refuge lay ahead. But the shadows grew longer, and the light retreated with every step. How much further until we found ourselves lost for good?

Riku's fingers brushed against mine as we pushed onward, a fleeting touch of warmth amidst the suffocating humidity. I glanced at her, catching the flicker of determination in her eyes, the set of her jaw. She knew, as I did, that we couldn't afford to falter now. Not with so many depending on us.

The dense foliage seemed to close in around us, a living, breathing entity that sought to swallow us whole. Each step required effort, each breath a struggle against the weight of the air itself. The twisted roots and tangled vines grabbed at our feet, threatening to trip us, to hold us back.

And then, without warning, the ground fell away.

I stumbled to a halt at the edge of a ravine, my heart lurching in my chest. Jagged rocks and steep walls stretched out before us, a gaping maw ready to devour the unwary. The roar of a distant river echoed up from the depths, a mocking reminder of the life-giving water that lay just out of reach.

"We have to find a way across." Riku's voice was steady, but I could hear the undercurrent of fear beneath the surface.

I nodded, my mind racing. We couldn't go back, couldn't risk retracing our steps through the treacherous jungle. But the path ahead seemed equally impossible. A single misstep, a moment of carelessness, and we would be lost to the abyss.

The others looked to me, their eyes pleading for guidance, for the strength to carry on. I swallowed hard, tasting the bitterness of my own doubts. How could I lead them when every decision felt like a gamble with their lives?

"We'll find a way," I said, the words sounding hollow even to my own ears. "We haven't come this far to give up now."

But as I stared into the yawning chasm before us, I couldn't help but wonder if we had already gone too far, if we had crossed a line from which there was no return. The ravine stretched out like a scar upon the earth, a wound that would never heal. And I feared that in leading them here, I had sealed our fate, condemned us to a slow, agonizing demise in the belly of the jungle.

The weight of their trust, their hope, settled upon my shoulders like a physical burden. I closed my eyes for a moment, seeking the strength to carry on, to be the leader they needed me to be. But in the darkness behind my eyelids, I saw only the faces of the dead, the ones I had failed. They whispered to me, their voices a haunting chorus that drowned out all else.

I opened my eyes, blinking against the harsh light of day. The ravine waited, patient and unyielding. And beyond it, the unknown, the promise of salvation or the certainty of damnation. There was only one way to find out which lay ahead.

"Let's go," I said, my voice a ragged whisper. "Watch your step and stay close. We'll make it through this together."

But even as I said the words, I couldn't quite bring myself to believe them. The jungle had a way of twisting the truth, of turning hope into despair. And as we began our treacherous descent into the ravine, I couldn't shake the feeling that we were walking willingly into the heart of darkness, into a place from which there would be no escape.

The vines cut into my palms, their rough fibers biting deep as I gripped them tight. My muscles strained, screaming in protest as I lowered myself down the steep face of the ravine. Above me, the others followed suit, their movements slow and cautious, their breaths coming in short, sharp gasps.

I chanced a glance below, instantly regretting it as vertigo swept over me. The bottom of the ravine was a dizzying distance away, the jagged rocks waiting eagerly to embrace anyone who slipped. I swallowed hard, forcing my gaze back to the wall in front of me.

"Don't look down," I called out, my voice echoing in the narrow space. "Just focus on your hands and feet. One step at a time."

But even as I spoke the words of encouragement, doubt gnawed at my mind. What if the vines couldn't hold our weight? What if one of us lost our grip, plummeting to a gruesome end? The thoughts circled like vultures, feeding on my fear.

Riku's voice drifted down from above, strained but determined. "We're almost there, Maikoru. Just a little further."

I clung to her words like a lifeline, drawing strength from her presence. She had always been the one to keep me grounded, to remind me of what mattered most. But now, with death lurking in every shadow, I wondered if even her light could pierce the darkness that threatened to consume us all.

My foot found a narrow ledge, and I paused to catch my breath. The air was thick and heavy, the humidity pressing down like a physical weight. Sweat poured down my face, stinging my eyes and blurring my vision.

"Keep moving," I urged, as much to myself as to the others. "We can't stay here."

And so we pressed on, descending deeper into the bowels of the earth. The walls closed in around us, the ravine narrowing until it felt like the very earth itself was trying to swallow us whole. My heart pounded in my chest, a frantic drumbeat that drowned out all other sounds.

At last, my feet touched solid ground. I stumbled forward, my legs trembling from the exertion. The others joined me one by one, their faces etched with relief and exhaustion.

But even as we gathered our strength, a new horror awaited. For in the depths of the ravine, the shadows stirred and shifted, and the moans of the undead echoed off the stone walls. We had escaped one danger, only to find ourselves in the midst of another.

And as the first rotting hand reached out from the darkness, I knew that our journey was far from over. The jungle had claimed us, and it would not let us go without a fight.

I steeled myself, gripping my weapon tighter as we ventured deeper into the heart of the jungle. The air grew thicker, the foliage pressing in on all sides until it felt like the very trees were reaching out to ensnare us.

"Watch your step," Riku whispered, her voice barely audible above the rustle of leaves. "The ground is treacherous here."

I nodded, scanning the undergrowth for any sign of movement. But the jungle was still, save for the occasional flutter of wings or the distant cry of some unknown creature.

We pushed onward, our steps growing heavier with each passing moment. Exhaustion weighed upon us like a physical burden, dragging at our limbs and clouding our minds. But we could not stop, could not rest. Not here, not now.

The trees pressed closer, their branches intertwining overhead until the sky was barely visible. The air grew thick and oppressive, the scent of decay and rot filling my nostrils.

"It's like the jungle is trying to suffocate us," Riku murmured, her voice tinged with fear.

I said nothing, but silently agreed. The weight of the jungle bore down upon us, a malevolent presence that seemed to watch our every move.

And then, just when I thought I could bear it no longer, the trees parted and we stumbled into a small clearing. The sun broke through the canopy, casting dappled shadows on the forest floor.

But even here, in this brief respite from the oppressive gloom, I could feel the jungle watching us, waiting. It was only a matter of time before it claimed us once more.

Suddenly, a rustling sound shattered the eerie stillness, causing us to freeze in our tracks. My heart pounded against my ribcage as my eyes darted through the dense foliage, searching for the source of the disturbance.

"What was that?" Riku whispered, her voice trembling with fear.

I raised a hand, silencing her. The sound came again, closer this time. A twig snapped, and the undergrowth parted slightly, as if something was pushing through it.

"Stay behind me," I murmured, tightening my grip on my weapon.

I took a step forward, my senses heightened, every nerve in my body on high alert. The jungle seemed to hold its breath, waiting for the inevitable confrontation.

And then I saw it. A flash of decaying flesh, a tattered remnant of clothing. The undead creature stumbled into view, its movements jerky and uncoordinated.

My breath caught in my throat, and for a moment, I was paralyzed by fear. The creature's eyes, once human but now glazed over with a milky white film, locked onto mine. It let out a guttural moan, a sound that chilled me to the bone.

"Maikoru..." Riku's voice was barely audible, but it snapped me out of my trance.

I raised my weapon, my hands shaking slightly. The creature took another step forward, its jaws snapping, a string of saliva hanging from its rotting teeth.

"We have to go," I said, my voice hoarse. "Now."

But even as the words left my lips, I knew it was too late. The creature lunged forward, its arms outstretched, its fingers curled into claws.

And in that moment, I knew that the jungle had finally claimed us, that we were nothing more than prey in this twisted game of survival. The sins of our past had finally caught up with us, and there was no escape from the horrors that lurked in the shadows.

We dove for cover, our hearts pounding in our chests as we pressed our backs against the thick trunks of the towering trees. The undead creature stumbled past, its gait unsteady, its senses dulled by the rot that had consumed its body.

I held my breath, the stench of decay filling my nostrils, a reminder of the fate that awaited us all. Beside me, Riku trembled, her eyes wide with fear. I reached out, my hand finding hers, a silent reassurance that we were in this together, no matter the cost.

The seconds ticked by, each one an eternity as we waited for the creature to pass. Its rasping breaths echoed in the stillness of the jungle, a haunting melody that would forever be etched into our memories.

Finally, the creature moved on, disappearing into the dense foliage, leaving us alone with our fear and the weight of our sins. We emerged from our hiding spots, our movements cautious, our senses heightened to the point of pain.

"We can't stay here," I said, my voice barely above a whisper. "We have to keep moving."

Riku nodded, her face pale, her eyes haunted by the horrors we had witnessed. We resumed our journey, our footsteps heavy with the knowledge that death lurked around every corner, waiting to claim us as its own.

The jungle closed in around us, the trees reaching out with gnarled branches, as if to ensnare us in their embrace. The air grew thicker, the humidity pressing down upon us like a physical weight, making each breath a struggle.

But still, we pushed on, driven by the primal need to survive, to outrun the ghosts of our past and the monsters that hunted us. We clung to each other, our bond the only thing that kept us from succumbing to the madness that threatened to consume us.

And as we walked, I couldn't shake the feeling that we were being watched, that the eyes of the jungle were upon us, judging us for the sins we had committed, the lives we had taken in the name of survival.

How long could we go on like this, I wondered, before the weight of our guilt dragged us down into the abyss, before the jungle claimed us as its own, and we became just another footnote in the endless cycle of life and death?

As we ventured deeper into the heart of the rainforest, a new sound began to mingle with the eerie chorus of the jungle—the distant roar of rushing water. It grew louder with each step, a siren's call that pulled us forward, promising salvation from the horrors that pursued us.

"Do you hear that?" Riku whispered, her voice barely audible above the cacophony of the forest. "It sounds like a waterfall."

I nodded, my throat too dry to speak. The thought of fresh water, of washing away the grime and the blood that caked our skin, was almost too much to bear. We quickened our pace, the promise of respite driving us onward.

The trees began to thin, the dense foliage giving way to a clearing that seemed to materialize out of the mist. And there, before us, was a sight that stole the breath from our lungs—a hidden waterfall, its cascading waters shimmering like diamonds in the dappled sunlight.

For a moment, we could only stare, transfixed by the beauty of the scene. It seemed almost too perfect, a mirage conjured by our desperate minds. But the cool mist that kissed our faces was real, the thundering roar of the water a tangible presence.

"Is this a dream?" Riku murmured, her voice tinged with awe and disbelief.

I shook my head, a faint smile tugging at the corners of my lips. "If it is, then let us hope we never wake up."

We approached the waterfall cautiously, our eyes scanning the surrounding area for any signs of danger. But there was nothing, only the gentle sway of the trees and the hypnotic rush of the water.

As we drew closer, I couldn't shake the feeling that there was something otherworldly about this place, as if it existed outside of time and space, untouched by the horrors that had ravaged the world beyond. It was a sanctuary, a fleeting glimpse of the beauty that still existed in this shattered world.

But even as we reveled in the moment, I knew that it couldn't last. The jungle was a cruel mistress, and she would not let us go so easily.

We had to savor this respite while we could, to gather our strength for the trials that lay ahead.

For in this world, there was no such thing as safety, no haven that could shelter us from the darkness that lurked within the hearts of men. We were all damned, cursed to wander this blighted earth until the last of us drew breath.

And yet, as I gazed upon the shimmering waters of the hidden waterfall, I couldn't help but feel a flicker of hope, a whisper of something that might have been redemption. Perhaps, in this fleeting moment of beauty, we could find the strength to carry on, to face the demons that haunted us and emerge from the shadows, forever changed.

As I emerged from the pool, rivulets of water cascading down my weary limbs, I turned to face my companions. Their faces were etched with a mix of exhaustion and relief, a testament to the trials we had endured.

"We can't stay here long," I said, my voice barely above a whisper. "The undead may have lost our scent for now, but they'll never stop hunting us."

Riku met my gaze, her eyes gleaming with a fierce determination. "We'll take what rest we can, then press on. We've come too far to give up now."

I nodded, feeling a surge of admiration for her unwavering spirit. In a world where hope was a fleeting commodity, Riku's strength was a beacon, guiding us through the darkness.

As the others set about refilling our water skins and tending to our wounds, I found myself drawn back to the waterfall, its hypnotic rhythm a siren song that called to the depths of my soul.

I closed my eyes, letting the sound wash over me, drowning out the constant thrum of fear that had become my constant companion. For a moment, I could almost forget the horrors that lurked beyond the veil of the jungle, the shambling corpses that hungered for our flesh.

But even as I lost myself in the moment, I couldn't shake the feeling that we were being watched, that some malevolent force was lurking just beyond the periphery of my vision, waiting for the perfect moment to strike.

It was a feeling I had come to know all too well, a sixth sense honed by countless brushes with death. And as I opened my eyes, scanning the dense foliage for any sign of movement, I knew that our respite was drawing to a close.

The jungle was a harsh mistress, and she would not be denied her due. We had to keep moving, to stay one step ahead of the horde that pursued us, even if it meant plunging deeper into the heart of darkness.

For in this world, there was no turning back, no escape from the fate that had been thrust upon us. We were the last of our kind, the survivors of a plague that had consumed the world, and our only hope lay in the bonds we had forged in the crucible of adversity.

As I turned to rejoin my companions, I felt a renewed sense of purpose, a grim determination to see this journey through to its bitter end. For better or worse, we were in this together, and we would not rest until we had found a way to reclaim the world that had been stolen from us.

The weight of leadership bore down upon my shoulders as I surveyed our ragtag band of survivors, their faces etched with the same weariness that I felt in my own bones. Riku, ever faithful, met my gaze with a flicker of understanding, a silent acknowledgment of the burden we shared.

"We should move on," I said, my voice low and steady. "We've lingered here too long already."

Nods of assent rippled through the group, a testament to the trust they had placed in me. It was a trust I feared I might one day betray, a fear that gnawed at the edges of my mind like a hungry rat.

But there was no time for doubts, no room for hesitation. The undead were relentless, driven by an insatiable hunger that knew no bounds. We had to be stronger, faster, smarter if we hoped to survive.

As we set off once more, the jungle closed in around us, a living, breathing entity that seemed to watch our every move with malevolent intent. The air was thick and heavy, laden with the sweet, cloying scent of decay.

I could feel the eyes of the others upon me, searching for some sign of weakness, some crack in the facade of strength I had so carefully cultivated. But I would not let them see the fear that lurked beneath the surface, the doubts that plagued my every waking moment.

For I knew that the moment I faltered, the moment I showed any hint of vulnerability, would be the moment that the horde descended upon us, tearing us limb from limb in a frenzy of gnashing teeth and grasping hands.

And so I pressed on, my steps never wavering, my eyes fixed upon the path ahead. The jungle may have been a cruel and unforgiving place, but it was the only home we had left, the only refuge from the horrors that haunted our every step.

In the end, it would be the strength of our will, the depth of our resolve, that would determine our fate. And I was determined to see us through, no matter the cost.

I watched as Riku knelt by the water's edge, her slender fingers cupping the cool, clear liquid and bringing it to her parched lips. For a moment, the hardness in her eyes softened, and I caught a glimpse of the girl she had once been, before the world had gone to hell.

"We can't stay here long," I said, my voice low and urgent. "We're too exposed."

Riku nodded, her gaze meeting mine. "I know. But we need this, Maikoru. We need a moment to breathe."

I couldn't argue with that. The weight of the journey, the constant fear and stress, had taken its toll on all of us. We were worn down, both physically and mentally, and this brief respite was a balm to our weary souls.

But even as we savored the peace of the hidden oasis, I couldn't shake the feeling that we were being watched. The hairs on the back of my neck prickled, and I scanned the surrounding foliage, searching for any sign of movement.

"We should go," I said, my voice barely above a whisper. "Something doesn't feel right."

Riku's eyes widened, and she rose to her feet, her hand instinctively reaching for the knife at her belt. "What is it?"

I shook my head, unable to put my finger on the source of my unease. "I don't know. But we can't afford to take any chances."

We gathered our belongings, our movements quick and efficient, driven by the urgency of our situation. As we prepared to set out once more, I caught Riku's eye, and she gave me a small, determined nod.

Together, we plunged back into the shadows of the rainforest, our senses heightened, our hearts pounding with a mixture of fear and adrenaline. Whatever lay ahead, we would face it together, bound by the unbreakable bonds of survival and shared trauma.

But even as we pushed forward, I couldn't shake the feeling that something was coming, something that would test us in ways we had never been tested before. And I knew, with a sinking certainty, that not all of us would make it out alive.

The hidden waterfall beckoned like an oasis amidst the nightmarish hellscape we now called home. Its gentle roar drowning out the distant moans and guttural cries. I collapsed beside Riku on the damp, moss-covered rocks, my blood-soaked machete clattering to the ground.

"I don't know how much longer I can keep going," Riku whispered, her haunted eyes staring vacantly at the cascading water.

My heart ached seeing the despair etched on her face, the same expression mirrored in my own weathered reflection. I took her trembling hand, our fingers lacing together, dirt and blood mingling. Her touch like a lifeline tethering me to this shattered world.

"We'll find a way, together. This can't be all there is..." My words rang hollow even to my own ears. Pretty lies to placate ourselves as everything crumbled to dust.

She turned to face me, tears carving paths through the grime on her cheeks. "I'm so scared, Kai. Scared of losing you, of being alone in this godforsaken place. Of becoming one of...them."

I pulled her close, breathing in her familiar scent beneath the layers of death and decay. She was my anchor, my reason to keep fighting, to keep clinging to the tattered shreds of my humanity.

"I won't let that happen. I'd die before I let them take you." The conviction in my voice surprised me. Maybe there was still some small scrap of strength left inside this broken shell.

Her lips curved into a ghost of a smile and she nestled closer, her head resting on my shoulder. In that moment, the horrors receded, held at bay by the fragile connection between us, this unbreakable bond forged in blood and heartache.

Yet even as I held her, whispering promises I wasn't sure I could keep, the ever-present dread coiled in my gut. The sins of my past, the choices that led to this hell on earth, forever haunting me. Tainting any chance of solace or redemption.

But for now, in this fleeting reprieve by the waterfall, I let myself believe the pretty lies. That hope still existed. That our love could overcome the gnawing darkness. That somehow, we'd make it out of this nightmare alive.

But I've learned the hard way that in this world, there are no fairytales. Only the cold, merciless grip of the undead, waiting to drag us all into the depths of oblivion.

We tarried by the waterfall until the light began to wane, the encroaching darkness a grim reminder of the dangers that lurked just outside our temporary sanctuary. Reluctantly, we rose to our feet, striking camp and gathering our meager belongings.

Hand in hand, we made our way back to the battered SUV that had become our home on wheels. The engine coughed to life, spewing out a plume of acrid smoke. Riku shut the passenger door, her hand lingered on mine, her emerald eyes filled with a thousand unspoken words.

As we pulled away, the waterfall disappeared behind us, its haunting beauty swallowed by the relentless jungle. A part of me knew we'd never find such peace again.

But for one fleeting moment, we'd had each other. And in this cursed wasteland, that was all we could hope for.

Ancient rainforest rushing past the cracked, grime-smeared windshield, I gripped the steering wheel, my knuckles whitening. The GPS could only do so much, its battered screen flickering like a dying candle. Trusting our lives to a fragile machine seemed like the epitome of folly.

Riku sensed my unease, her hand finding mine again. Her touch, always cool, sent a shiver down my spine. A ghostly reminder of the things that lurked in the shadows. The things that craved warm, beating hearts.

We drove in tense silence, the only sound the growl of the engine and the steady patter of rain against the roof. The rainforest pressed in from all sides, a living, breathing mass of greenery that seemed to mock our futile attempts at survival.

As night fell, we set up camp deep within the tangled embrace of the trees. The rain had eased to a drizzle, but the dampness seeped into our very bones. Riku huddled close to me, seeking warmth and solace. I wrapped my arms around her, trying to ignore the chilling certainty that our time together was borrowed.

As the fire crackled, casting flick ering shadows on the ancient trunks, I allowed myself a moment of respite. It was fleeting, but in that stolen

Writer's Response:

moment, we were not just a desperate scribe and his undead companion. We were two people, clinging to each other in the face of insurmountable odds. And for this one night, in the depths of the rainforest, we were still human.

As we settled down to sleep, Riku's cool fingers intertwined with mine, her shallow breaths the only evidence of her undead state. I knew that the slightest lapse in vigilance could mean our end. But even so, I let my eyes slide closed, willing myself to find an ephemeral reprieve from the horrors of this world.

In my dreams, the zombies lurked, their rotting forms shambling through the once-vibrant streets of Tokyo. But even in my sleep, Riku was there, her icy grip on my hand an assurance that we were in this together.

Hours passed in the blink of an eye, and when the eastern sky began to lighten, I awoke with a start. The fire had burned down to embers, and Riku slept peacefully beside me. Miraculously

I knew better, of course. I'd seen too much to indulge in such naivety. But as the zombies roamed the wasteland, their moans a macabre lullaby, I allowed myself the luxury of pretending.

Pretending that we had a future.

Pretending that we could outrun the monsters, both outside and within.

Pretending that there was a tomorrow.

Dawn would bring the reckoning, the harsh light of day shattering our illusions like so much broken glass. Until then, I clung to her, to this fleeting glimpse of normalcy.

For once, let me be selfish.

Let me believe in the lie.

For tomorrow, we fight again.

Tomorrow, we die.

But tonight... tonight, we were invincible.

Untouchable.

And that was enough.

At least, until the sunrise stole our dreams away.

The lush scent of the rain-soaked earth mingled with the warmth radiating from our entwined bodies, a heady perfume that dulled the ever-present stench of decay. In this stolen moment, the world narrowed to the thrum of her heartbeat against my chest, the featherlight caress of her breath on my skin.

I closed my eyes, letting the sensations wash over me, heightening every point of contact between us. The cool mist from the waterfall, the silken strands of her hair brushing my cheek, the supple curves of her body molding to mine. Each touch, each shared breath, a defiant proclamation that we were still alive, still human.

"Do you remember," she murmured, her lips grazing my ear, "the promises we made, before all this? The dreams we had?"

A bitter chuckle escaped me. Dreams. Fragile wisps of longing, shattered by the cruel reality we now inhabited. Yet I clung to them still, these phantom echoes of a life that no longer existed.

"I remember." My fingers traced the delicate line of her jaw, committing every detail to memory. "A house by the sea. Waking up to the sound of the waves, your head on my chest. Growing old together, surrounded by the people we love."

"We can still have that." Her voice wavered, but there was a fierce determination in her eyes. "We'll find a way. We'll make a new life, a new home. Together."

I wanted to believe her, to lose myself in the beautiful fantasy she wove. But the weight of my past, the burden of my sins, pressed down on me, an inescapable reminder of the man I used to be. The man who had set this apocalypse in motion.

"I don't deserve that kind of future. Not after everything I've done." The words tasted like ashes on my tongue.

She cupped my face in her hands, forcing me to meet her gaze. "We've all done things we regret. Things we had to do to survive. That doesn't define who we are."

A part of me yearned to embrace her absolution, to let her faith in me wash away the stains on my soul. But I knew better. The blood on my hands would never truly be clean.

Still, I nodded, mustering a smile that felt like a lie. "You're right. We'll find a way."

She sealed my words with a kiss, a searing promise that branded my heart. In that moment, with the taste of her on my lips and the scent of the earth enveloping us, I could almost believe that redemption was possible. That our love could be the light that guided us through this endless darkness.

But even as I surrendered to the intoxicating rush of her touch, a part of me knew the truth. There was no escaping the horrors that plagued us, no outrunning the ghosts of our past. We were forever marked by this apocalypse, our souls stained by the blood we'd spilled and the lives we'd taken.

Yet for now, in this fleeting oasis of peace, I let myself pretend. That our whispered promises held the power to reshape reality. That our shared dreams could become more than just wishful thinking. That the warmth of her body against mine could chase away the chill of the grave that awaited us.

The distant moans of the undead tore through the thin veil of our sanctuary, a haunting reminder of the nightmares that lurked just beyond the waterfall's mist. Riku tensed in my arms, her breath hitching as the eerie sounds grew louder, carried on the wind like a sinister chorus.

"They're getting closer," she whispered, her voice trembling with a fear I knew all too well. "We can't stay here much longer."

I tightened my embrace, silently willing the world to fade away, to grant us just a few more moments of solace. But the rustling of leaves and the snapping of twigs shattered that fragile illusion, each sound a jarring reminder of the relentless hunger that pursued us.

"I know," I murmured, my words heavy with the weight of our reality. "But for now, let's just hold on to this. To us."

In the face of the encroaching darkness, we clung to each other like two drowning souls, desperate for a lifeline. Her heartbeat echoed against my chest, a steady rhythm that seemed to whisper, "You are not alone."

And in that moment, I felt it—a flicker of strength amidst the despair, a glimmer of hope in the shadow of death. With Riku by my side, I could almost believe that we had a chance, that our love could be the anchor that kept us from drifting into the abyss.

But even as I savored the warmth of her skin and the softness of her lips, I couldn't shake the icy tendrils of dread that coiled in my gut. The moans grew louder, the rustling more insistent, and I knew that our reprieve was drawing to a close.

We were living on borrowed time, stealing moments of solace in a world that had no mercy. And as much as I wanted to lose myself in the illusion of safety, I knew that we couldn't hide forever.

The zombies were coming, and we would have to face them once more. But for now, in this fleeting instant of peace, I let myself believe that our love could conquer all. Even if it was nothing more than a beautiful lie.

Reluctantly, I loosened my embrace, feeling the chill of the rain-soaked air rush between us. Riku's eyes met mine, a silent understanding passing between us. We had to go back, to face the nightmares that lurked beyond the sanctuary of the waterfall.

"We can't stay here forever," I whispered, my voice barely audible above the cascading water. "The others need us."

Riku nodded, her jaw clenching with determination. "I know. But we'll face it together, no matter what comes."

She reached out, her fingers grazing my cheek in a final, lingering touch. The warmth of her skin seared into my memory, a talisman against the horrors to come.

We rose from our secluded spot, the damp earth clinging to our clothes like a reminder of the brief peace we had stolen. My heart ached with the weight of our love, a bittersweet pain that I knew would be my only comfort in the days ahead.

As we turned to leave, I caught a glimpse of our reflection in the rippling pool—two figures, battered and weary, but bound together by an unbreakable bond. In that moment, I knew that our love would be the beacon that guided us through the darkness, the flame that kept the shadows at bay.

Hand in hand, we stepped back into the treacherous embrace of the rainforest, our hearts heavy with the knowledge of the trials that awaited us. But beneath the fear and the sorrow, a new resolve burned bright—a determination to protect each other and the fragile remnants of our tribe.

We had tasted the sweetness of love in a world gone mad, and we would fight to our last breath to keep that flame alive. Even if it meant facing the armies of the undead, we would do it together, bound by a love that refused to die.

The dense foliage enveloped us, its eerie silence broken only by the distant moans of the undead. Each step was a reminder of the dangers that lurked in the shadows, the twisted remnants of humanity that hungered for our flesh.

I tightened my grip on Riku's hand, drawing strength from his presence. "Do you think we'll ever find a place where we can be safe?" I whispered, my voice barely audible above the rustling leaves.

Riku's eyes met mine, a flicker of hope amidst the darkness. "As long as we have each other, we'll always have a sanctuary," he murmured, his words a balm to my battered soul.

We pressed on, the weight of our weapons a familiar burden against our backs. The rainforest seemed to close in around us, its twisted branches reaching out like grasping fingers. But even as the darkness deepened, I could feel the warmth of Riku's love guiding me forward, a light in the endless night.

In the depths of my mind, I could still taste his kiss, feel the heat of his skin against mine. Those stolen moments by the waterfall had etched themselves into my very being, a talisman against the despair that threatened to consume me.

We moved as one, our steps perfectly in sync, our senses attuned to the slightest hint of danger. The rainforest may have been a living nightmare, but with Riku by my side, I knew we could face whatever horrors lay ahead.

For in this world of death and decay, our love was the one thing that remained pure and unblemished—a testament to the resilience of the human spirit, and a promise of the life we would build together, even amidst the ruins of civilization.

As the days bled into weeks, our love only grew stronger, a defiant flame against the encroaching darkness. In the midst of the chaos and carnage, we found solace in each other's arms, our whispered promises a lifeline in a world gone mad.

"Do you remember the first time we met?" Riku asked, his voice barely audible over the distant groans of the undead.

I smiled, the memory a fleeting warmth in the chill of the night. "How could I forget? You were like a beacon of hope in a sea of despair."

He pulled me closer, his strong arms a fortress against the horrors that lurked just beyond the treeline. "And you were the most beautiful thing I'd ever seen. Even covered in blood and grime, you shone like a star."

We clung to each other, our love a shield against the relentless onslaught of death and decay. In the darkest moments, when all seemed lost, it was the thought of our future together that kept us going, a glimmer of hope amidst the bleak reality of our existence.

But even as our bond deepened, the world around us continued to crumble. The undead seemed to multiply with each passing day, their moans a constant reminder of the fate that awaited us should we falter.

"We can't go on like this forever," I whispered, my voice thick with the weight of our shared burden. "Sooner or later, they'll catch up to us."

Riku's grip tightened, his eyes blazing with a fierce determination. "Then we'll face them together. We've come too far to give up now."

And so we pressed on, our love a beacon of hope in a world consumed by darkness. Though the future remained uncertain, one thing was clear: as long as we had each other, we would never stop fighting for the life we dreamed of, even if it meant facing the horrors of the apocalypse head-on.

My words cut through the silent air, heavy with the stench of fear and desperation. "We cannot afford to be divided," I said, my eyes scanning the haggard faces before me. "Our strength lies in our unity. In our shared purpose—survival."

A murmur rippled through the group, a mix of reluctant nods and averted gazes. I could feel their doubt pressing against me like a physical force, threatening to shatter the fragile hold I had on their loyalty.

I stepped forward, my hand resting on the hilt of my katana. "Each of you has a role to play. A responsibility to fulfill." I turned to Riku, her dark eyes glinting with a fierce determination that mirrored my own. "Riku, you will lead a scouting party to search for food and supplies."

She nodded curtly, her lips pressed into a thin line. I could see the weight of the task settling on her shoulders, but I knew she would not falter.

Next, I addressed Hana, the young healer whose gentle hands belied a steely resolve. "Hana, you will tend to the wounded and ensure our medical supplies are well-stocked." She bowed her head in assent, her delicate features etched with a quiet strength.

I continued assigning tasks, my voice steady and unwavering. Kenji would reinforce our defenses, shoring up the walls and fortifying our position. Akio would take charge of rationing our dwindling food stores, ensuring that each person received their fair share. And Yumi, with her keen eye and steady aim, would stand watch over the perimeter.

As I spoke, I could feel the restlessness in the group begin to dissipate, replaced by a sense of purpose. They had direction now, a reason to push forward through the unrelenting darkness that threatened to consume us all.

But even as I watched them disperse to their assigned duties, I couldn't shake the nagging doubt that gnawed at the edges of my mind. How long could I keep them together? How long before the cracks in our fragile alliance gave way under the weight of the horrors we faced?

I shook my head, banishing the dark thoughts. I had to be strong. For them. For all of us. The specter of my past sins loomed large in my mind, a constant reminder of the price of failure. I would not let them down. Not again.

I turned my gaze to the horizon, where the sun struggled to pierce the thick veil of ominous clouds. Beyond lay a land of myth and whispered promises, as intangible as the faded memories of a lost world. But it was all we had left to cling to—a fragile hope in the face of unrelenting despair.

My grip tightened on my katana, the cool weight of the steel a comforting presence at my side. Whatever lay ahead, I would face it. For the sake of those who followed me, I had to.

As I surveyed the camp, a voice cut through the uneasy silence. Takeshi, one of the younger warriors, stepped forward, his eyes blazing with defiance.

"Maikoru, how can you expect us to follow you when all we've known is death and despair since you took charge?" His words were laced with venom, each syllable a dagger aimed at my heart.

The others murmured their agreement, a rising tide of discontent that threatened to sweep away the fragile order I had fought so hard to maintain. I felt the weight of their doubts pressing down upon me, suffocating in its intensity.

I met Takeshi's gaze, my own eyes hardening with resolve. "I understand your fears, Takeshi. We've all suffered, all lost more than we ever thought possible. But we cannot let our pain and uncertainty divide us. Not now, when our very survival hangs in the balance."

My words did little to quell the rising tension. Others began to voice their own doubts, their own frustrations. Each accusation was a blow to my already battered soul, a reminder of the heavy burden I carried.

I fought to maintain my composure, even as the ghosts of my past whispered their condemnation in my ear. How could I lead them when I myself was haunted by the specter of my own failures?

But I couldn't let them see my weakness. Not now, when they needed me to be strong. I drew in a deep breath, steadying myself against the onslaught of their anger and fear.

"I know the path ahead is uncertain," I said, my voice low and intense. "But we cannot let that uncertainty tear us apart. We are all that stands between ourselves and oblivion. If we falter now, if we let our doubts and fears consume us, then all that we have fought for, all that we have lost, will have been for nothing."

I let my gaze sweep over the gathered survivors, meeting each of their eyes in turn. "I don't pretend to have all the answers. But I do know this: we are stronger together than we ever could be apart. Our survival, our very existence, depends on our ability to stand united in the face of the darkness that threatens to consume us all."

The weight of my words hung heavy in the air, a palpable presence that seemed to press down upon us all. For a long moment, no one spoke. Then, slowly, the tension began to ease, replaced by a grim determination.

They knew, as I did, that the road ahead would be fraught with peril. But they also knew that we had no choice but to walk it, to cling to the faint hope of a better tomorrow, no matter how distant it might seem.

As the group dispersed, returning to their assigned tasks with renewed purpose, I felt a flicker of something I had not felt in a long time: hope. It was a fragile thing, as delicate as a candle flame in a tempest. But it was there, a tiny spark of light amidst the suffocating darkness.

I knew that the trials ahead would test us all, that the ghosts of our pasts would continue to haunt our every step. But for now, in this moment, we were united. And that, perhaps, was the greatest weapon we had against the unrelenting horror that sought to claim us all.

I turned to Riku, my eyes searching her face for any sign of hesitation or doubt. "You understand the importance of this mission, don't you?" My voice was low, almost a whisper, as if I feared the very walls might overhear our conversation.

She met my gaze unflinchingly, her jaw set with determination. "I do," she replied, her words laced with a quiet strength that belied her slender frame. "We cannot survive on hope alone. If there is food to be found, I will find it."

I nodded, a flicker of pride burning in my chest. Riku had always been one of the strongest among us, a survivor in every sense of the word. If anyone could navigate the treacherous landscape that lay beyond our walls, it was her.

"Take only a small group with you," I instructed, my mind already racing with the logistics of the mission. "Move swiftly and silently.

Avoid confrontation if you can, but do not hesitate to defend yourselves if necessary."

Riku inclined her head in acknowledgment, her eyes glinting with a fierce resolve. "We will not fail," she vowed, her words a solemn oath that hung heavy in the air between us.

As I watched her gather her team, a sense of unease coiled in the pit of my stomach. The world beyond our walls was a savage place, a twisted mockery of the life we had once known. Every venture into that unforgiving landscape was a dance with death, a gamble that could end in blood and sorrow.

But what choice did we have? To remain within the confines of our sanctuary was to invite a slow, lingering demise. We needed food, and the only way to obtain it was to brave the dangers that lurked beyond our borders.

I turned my attention to the task at hand, rallying those who remained to fortify our defenses. We worked with a grim efficiency, each of us acutely aware of the stakes we faced. Every barrier we erected, every trap we set, was a silent prayer to whatever gods might still be listening, a desperate plea for just one more day of survival.

As the sun began to dip below the horizon, painting the sky in hues of blood and fire, I found myself standing atop the ramparts, my gaze fixed on the treeline beyond. Somewhere out there, Riku and her team were fighting for our future, risking their lives in a world gone mad.

I closed my eyes, my heart heavy with the knowledge of the sacrifices we had made, and those we would inevitably make still. In this new world, hope was a luxury we could ill afford. But still, I clung to it, a fragile lifeline in a sea of despair.

For without hope, what were we? Just another horde of the damned, wandering the ruins of a world we no longer recognized, waiting for the inevitable end to claim us all.

The silence was shattered by a piercing scream, a sound that chilled me to the very marrow of my bones. My eyes snapped open, my hand instinctively reaching for the weapon at my side. The others, too, had heard the cry, their faces etched with a mix of fear and grim determination.

We moved as one, a well-oiled machine born of necessity and desperation. The barricades we had so carefully constructed groaned under the weight of the onslaught, the relentless tide of undead flesh crashing against them like waves upon a rocky shore.

I fought with a fury I had never known, my blade slicing through rotten flesh and shattered bone. Beside me, my companions did the same, their weapons flashing in the fading light like the last defiant sparks of a dying fire.

But for every one we felled, two more seemed to take its place. They came at us from all sides, an endless stream of nightmares made flesh. I heard the screams of the wounded, the wet, choking gurgles of the dying, and I knew that our time was running out.

"Hold the line!" I shouted, my voice raw with desperation. "We must hold!"

But even as the words left my lips, I saw the barricades begin to give way, the rotten hands of the undead clawing at the gaps, their hungry moans filling the air.

And then, through the chaos and the terror, a single thought crystallized in my mind, sharp and cold as a shard of ice. Riku. She was out there still, fighting her own battles, unaware of the horror that had befallen us.

I had sent her to her death, I realized, a bitter bile rising in my throat. In my arrogance, my desperation to prove myself a leader, I had condemned her and those with her to a fate worse than any I could imagine.

The weight of that knowledge threatened to crush me, to drag me down into the waiting arms of the horde. But I pushed it aside, burying it deep within the recesses of my mind. There would be time enough for guilt, for recrimination, if any of us survived the night.

For now, there was only the fight, the desperate struggle to hold on to the last fading embers of our humanity in the face of an enemy that knew no mercy, no reason, no end.

And so I fought, my blade singing its mournful song as it cleaved through the ranks of the undead. I fought for Riku, for the ones we had lost, for the fragile hope of a future that seemed to slip further away with each passing moment.

I fought, even as the barricades crumbled and the horde poured in like a black tide, even as the screams of my companions were swallowed by the roar of the undead.

I fought, because in the end, it was all I had left. The last, defiant act of a man who had already lost everything, but who refused to surrender, even in the face of the abyss.

And as the world around me descended into a maelstrom of blood and terror, I clung to that defiance, that stubborn, unyielding core of who I was.

For in the end, it was all that separated me from the monsters at our door.

The battle raged on, a dance of death and desperation set against the backdrop of a world gone mad. I lost myself in the rhythm of the fight, my sword an extension of my will as it carved a path through the sea of grasping hands and gnashing teeth.

But even as I fought, I could feel the weight of our losses pressing down upon me, a burden that grew heavier with each fallen comrade. We had paid a steep price for our survival, and I knew that the toll would only continue to rise.

As if summoned by my darkening thoughts, Riku and her team emerged from the forest, their faces grim and their steps heavy with exhaustion. They carried with them a meager supply of food, barely enough to sustain us for a few days, and I could see the despair etched into the lines of their faces.

But it was the injuries that caught my eye, the bloody bandages and the limping gaits that spoke of the price they had paid for their scavenging. They had faced their own horrors out there in the wild, and I could only imagine the scars that they would carry with them, both physical and mental.

As they approached, I felt a surge of guilt, a bitter reminder of my own failings as a leader. I had sent them out there, into the jaws of danger, and now they had returned, battered and broken, with little to show for their efforts.

But there was no time for recriminations, no time for self-pity. We had to keep moving, to press on in the face of impossible odds, or else all of our sacrifices would be for nothing.

And so I called for a moment of silence, a brief respite in the chaos to honor the fallen and to remind ourselves of what we fought for. We stood there, heads bowed and hearts heavy, as the weight of our losses pressed down upon us like a physical thing.

But even in that moment of grief, I could feel the eyes of the others upon me, searching for some sign of hope, some glimmer of a future beyond the nightmare that had become our reality.

And so I stood tall, my voice steady as I spoke the words that I knew they needed to hear. "We will endure," I said, my gaze sweeping across the battered and bloodied faces of my companions. "We will survive, and we will find a way to build a new life from the ashes of the old."

It was a lie, of course. A pretty fiction spun to keep us going, to give us something to cling to in the face of the abyss. But in that moment, it was a lie that we all needed to believe.

For in the end, hope was all we had left, a fragile flame flickering in the darkness of a world gone mad. And I would be damned if I let that flame go out, even if it meant lying to myself and to those who looked to me for leadership.

The meeting was a somber affair, a gathering of the broken and the damned. We huddled together in the dimly lit room, our faces etched with the scars of a thousand battles, our eyes haunted by the memory of those we had lost.

I listened as they spoke, each voice a trembling whisper in the stillness. They spoke of their fears, their doubts, their desperate longing for a future that seemed forever out of reach. And through it all, I nodded and murmured empty platitudes, my mind racing as I struggled to find some way to hold us together.

But even as I listened, I could feel a growing sense of unease, a prickling at the back of my neck that set my teeth on edge. Something was wrong, some subtle shift in the air that I couldn't quite put my finger on.

And then, in a moment of pure, crystalline horror, I heard it. The sound of shattering glass, the guttural moans of the undead as they poured through the windows like a tide of rotting flesh.

Chaos erupted, screams mingling with the snarls of the zombies as we scrambled for our weapons. I leapt to my feet, my heart pounding in my chest as I drew my katana from its sheath.

"To arms!" I cried, my voice ringing out above the din. "Fight for your lives, for each other, for the future we still dare to dream of!"

And with that, I charged forward, my blade flashing in the flickering light as I met the first of the undead head-on. The battle was a blur of blood and steel, a desperate struggle for survival against an enemy that knew no fear, no mercy.

But even as I fought, I could feel a strange sense of clarity washing over me, a cold, sharp focus that cut through the terror and the chaos like a knife. This was my purpose, my calling, the reason I had been spared in a world gone mad.

I was a leader, a protector, a guardian of the last flickering embers of humanity. And I would fight to my last breath to keep that flame alive, to guide my people through the darkness and into the light beyond.

As the last of the zombies fell, I turned to face my companions, my chest heaving with exertion. They stood there, bloodied and battered, but alive, their eyes wide with a mixture of fear and awe.

"Do you see now?" I asked, my voice low and intense. "Do you understand the strength that lies within each of you, the power that comes from standing together against the darkness?"

I stepped forward, meeting each of their gazes in turn. "We are a family, bound by more than just the need to survive. We are the guardians of a future worth fighting for, a dream that refuses to die."

I could see the doubt and uncertainty in their eyes beginning to fade, replaced by a growing sense of determination. They nodded, their grips tightening on their weapons as they stood a little taller, a little straighter.

"From this moment on, we are no longer just survivors," I declared, my voice ringing out in the stillness. "We are warriors, united in purpose and in heart. We will face whatever horrors this world may throw at us, and we will emerge victorious."

I began to move among them, assigning new roles and responsibilities based on the strengths and skills I had seen displayed in the heat of battle. To Riku, I gave the task of scouting, her keen eyes and quick reflexes making her the perfect choice to keep watch for danger. To Takeshi, I entrusted the training of our fighters, knowing that his courage and tenacity would inspire them to new heights of skill and bravery.

And to the others, I gave the duties of foraging, crafting, and tending to the needs of our little community, each role vital in its own way to our continued survival.

As I spoke, I could feel a new sense of purpose taking hold, a renewed determination to press on in the face of all obstacles. We had been tested, and we had emerged stronger, more united than ever before.

The road ahead would be long and treacherous, fraught with perils both known and unknown. But I knew, with a certainty that bordered on madness, that we would endure, that we would find a way to carve out a future from the ashes of the past.

For we were the last hope of humanity, the flickering candle in the endless night. And we would burn bright, no matter how deep the darkness grew.

I gazed out at the faces before me, a sea of doubt and uncertainty, yet also of grim resolve. They were my people, my responsibility, and I would not let them down.

"We have faced the worst that this world has to offer," I said, my voice ringing out through the stillness of the night. "We have stared into the abyss, and we have not flinched. We have lost friends, loved ones, but we have not lost ourselves."

I paused, letting the weight of my words sink in. "And now, we stand on the precipice of a new beginning. A chance to build something better, something stronger than what came before."

I could see the glimmer of hope in their eyes, the spark of determination that refused to be extinguished. They were ready, I realized, ready to follow me to the ends of the earth and beyond.

"Tomorrow, we set out for the fabled land," I declared, my heart swelling with a fierce, unyielding pride. "We will face challenges, dangers, but we will face them together. As one people, one family, bound by blood and sacrifice."

The mood shifted, a palpable resolve settling over the group like a weight. They knew, as I did, that the path ahead would be fraught with peril. But they also knew that there was no turning back, no other choice but to press forward.

As the meeting dispersed, I caught Riku's eye, saw the flicker of understanding pass between us. She knew, perhaps better than anyone, the burden of leadership, the weight of responsibility that rested upon my shoulders.

But she also knew, as I did, that we would bear that weight together. That we would stand side by side, come what may, until our final breath.

The night grew deep, the shadows lengthening, but I felt no fear. For I knew that we were ready, that we had been forged in the crucible of this apocalypse, tempered by the fires of adversity.

And we would not be broken.

The stench of death clings to my nostrils as we creep through the suffocating rainforest. My heartbeat pounds in my ears, drowning out the eerie silence that blankets this godforsaken place. I clutch my machete and pistol, a slick sheen of sweat coating my hands despite the damp chill in the air.

"Eyes sharp," I whisper to the others, my voice a hoarse rasp. "Those rotting bastards could be anywhere."

Akira nods grimly, her dark eyes darting between the tangled vines and thick foliage, bow at the ready. Beside her, Kenji grips his baseball bat, jaw clenched tight.

We move as ghosts, careful to avoid the grasping undergrowth, fearing any sound may betray our presence to the abominations that haunt these woods.

Each step a delicate dance, choreographed by terror, propelled by the desperate need to survive. To keep breathing, against all odds, in a world gone mad.

My mind wanders unbidden to memories of before - before the dead rose, before everything fell apart. The faces of those I failed swim behind my eyes. The weight of their blood forever staining my hands.

I shake my head, forcing the ghosts back to their dark corners. Now is not the time for mourning. The dead are gone...but the undead remain. And I'll be damned if I let them claim anyone else.

A branch snaps.

We freeze, hardly daring to breathe. I raise a fist, scanning the trees for any sign of movement. Seconds stretch into agonizing eternities.

Then I see it. A shambling figure in the distance, lurching drunkenly between the shadows and shafts of wan light piercing the canopy. Even from here, I can make out the grotesque angle of its neck, the gaping holes where eyes used to be.

My blood runs cold.

"Get down," I hiss. "And pray it hasn't caught our scent."

We crouch amid the damp ferns, muscles coiled tight, pulses thrumming, as the nightmarish thing staggers closer...and closer still. An involuntary shudder runs down my spine.

Please, keep moving. Pass us by. Just a few more steps and-

The zombie pauses. Sniffs the air. Then slowly, horribly, its head swivels in our direction, rotten jaw yawning wide in a mockery of a grin.

My stomach drops. It knows we're here. And it's not alone. More shadowy shapes detach from the trees, their rasping moans rising in a blood-chilling chorus. Coming for us.

My hand tightens on my machete as I meet Akira's terrified gaze.

Dear God...into what fresh hell have I led us now?

A strangled cry rises in my throat, but I choke it back. Can't let fear take hold. Not now. Swallowing hard, I risk a glance over my shoulder at the others — ashen faces, wide eyes. Waiting for me to act. To save us.

"When I give the signal," I whisper hoarsely, "run like hell. Stay together. Don't look back."

Miko opens her mouth to argue, but I silence her with a sharp shake of my head. No time for debate. The undead are almost upon us, their putrid stench filling my nostrils, making me gag.

I suck in a deep, shuddering breath.

"Now!"

We burst from the undergrowth, startling the zombies. For a split second, they hesitate — all the opening I need. I lunge forward, my machete flashing as it bites deep into decaying flesh, sending a spray of black ichor through the air.

The creature crumples, but there are more behind it. Too many. They grasp at me with rotting fingers, yellowed teeth gnashing. I twist away, my heart jackhammering against my ribs.

"Go! I'll hold them off!"

The others race ahead as I dance between grasping hands and snapping jaws, my blade a silver arc, felling another fiend, then another. But it's not enough. Never enough. They just keep coming, a relentless tide of putrescence.

And then, from the corner of my eye, I see it. A flash of color amid the eternal grey and brown.

A tent. Tattered and faded but unmistakable. The remnants of a camp.

Hope surges through me, wild and desperate. If there was a camp, then maybe, just maybe...

"There!" I shout, pointing with my dripping machete. "We'll make our stand!"

I pivot and sprint after the others, the zombies close on my heels, their growls echoing in my ears. Lungs burning, muscles screaming, I put on a final burst of speed and-

We're through, stumbling into the clearing, the undead seconds behind us. But it's enough. It has to be.

I spin to face our pursuers as they stagger into the open, lips peeled back in soulless grimaces.

"Come on then, you bastards," I snarl, raising my blade high. "Let's dance."

God forgive me. I never meant for it to come to this...

With trembling fingers, I reach into the weathered pouch, hardly daring to breathe. The parchment crackles as I withdraw it, brittle and delicate as a whispered prayer.

A map. Dear God, a map.

My eyes devour the faded lines, the cryptic symbols, the promises of sanctuary. Tears blur the ink, making it run like blood.

Is this it? The key to our salvation? Or merely another false hope, another cruel jape in this cosmic jest?

I trace the route with a shaking hand, committing each twist and turn to memory. The others crowd around me, their faces gaunt and haunted, eyes glinting with desperate hunger.

"What is it?" Aiko whispers, her voice hoarse from disuse. "Maikoru, what have you found?"

I meet her gaze, seeing the fragile flicker of hope there, the unspoken plea. I want to lie, to spare her the crushing weight of disappointment. But I can't. Not anymore.

"A map," I rasp, my throat tight. "To a place without the scourge. A land of plenty, beyond the reach of the undead."

Futaba scoffs, her scarred lip twisting. "Another fairy tale. How many have we chased, only to find more death, more despair?"

"No," I snap, the conviction in my voice surprising even me. "This is different. This is real."

I hold up the map, the parchment crackling like old bones. "Look at it! The landmarks, the distances...it all fits. This is our chance, our one shot at a future."

Silence descends, heavy with unspoken doubts and fears. I see them warring on their faces, the desperate yearning for hope, the terror of having it shattered once more.

"Please," I whisper, my voice cracking. "Trust me. Just one more time."

And in that moment, I feel the weight of all my sins, all my failures, pressing down upon me like a physical thing. The lives I've taken, the ones I've failed to save...They haunt me, a legion of ghosts, their blood forever staining my hands.

But this...this is my chance for redemption. To lead them to safety, to carve out a piece of light in this endless darkness.

I will not fail them. Not again.

Even if it costs me everything.

My heart pounds as I watch them, their faces etched with the scars of our shared trauma. Futaba, her eyes hard and cynical, a map of pain carved into her skin. Kazuki, his broad shoulders slumped with the weight of too many losses. And little Hana, her innocence long since shattered, clutching her doll like a lifeline.

They are my family, my reason for fighting, for enduring the unendurable. And yet, I know I ask the impossible of them. To believe, when belief has brought nothing but heartache. To hope, when hope is a cruel mirage in this wasteland.

"Maikoru..." Kazuki's voice is heavy, laden with the weariness of a thousand battles. "We've been down this road before. Chasing dreams, only to find nightmares."

I nod, swallowing past the lump in my throat. "I know. God, I know. But this time...this time is different."

I step forward, the map trembling in my hands. "Look at the details, the precision. This isn't some hastily scrawled fantasy. This is real, tangible. A chance at a life beyond mere survival."

Hana's small voice pipes up, achingly fragile. "A life without monsters?"

I kneel before her, taking her tiny hands in mine. "Yes, sweetheart. A life without fear, without the constant stench of death. A place where you can grow, learn, be a child again."

Futaba's harsh laugh cuts through the air. "Pretty words, Maikoru. But words won't keep the undead from our throats. How do we know this so-called haven even exists?"

I meet her gaze unflinchingly, letting my conviction blaze forth. "We don't. But what's the alternative? To stay here, scavenging scraps, waiting for the day our luck runs out? Is that living?"

I stand, facing them all, my voice ringing with a passion I'd thought long dead. "This map is more than lines on paper. It's a lifeline, a promise of something better. And I will follow it, even if I have to walk through hell itself."

I pause, my chest heaving with the force of my emotion. "But I can't do it alone. I need you, all of you. Not just to survive, but to live. To hope."

The silence stretches, taut and brittle. I see the war raging behind their eyes, fear grappling with the desperate yearning for something more.

And then, slowly, Kazuki nods. "Okay, Maikoru. Okay. We're with you."

Futaba sighs, her shoulders sagging in resignation. "Not like we have anything to lose. Except our lives, of course."

Hana simply squezes my hand, her eyes shining with a fragile trust that breaks my heart even as it mends it.

I breathe out, dizzy with relief and a sudden, fierce joy. "Then it's decided. We leave at dawn, before the sun wakes the horrors."

As we prepare, a grim determination settles over us, the weight of our choice hanging heavy in the air. But beneath it, a flicker of something long forgotten:

Hope.

Treacherous, agonizing hope.

And may whatever gods remain have mercy on us all.

The night passes in a restless haze, my mind churning with visions of what lies ahead. I stare at the map, its faded lines seared into my eyes, a talisman against the encroaching darkness.

Dawn breaks, cold and merciless. We gather our meager possessions, the weight of our past lives discarded like shed skin. The forest looms before us, a sentient thing, hungry and waiting.

I lead the way, the map clutched in my sweaty palm. The others follow, a ragged procession of lost souls, bound by desperation and a fragile thread of trust.

We walk, and walk, the hours blurring into an endless march. The trees press in, their branches grasping, their roots eager to trip and ensnare. The air hangs thick and heavy, the silence broken only by the rasp of our breath and the crunch of our footsteps.

And then, a sound. A groan, low and guttural, a perversion of humanity. My heart clenches, my hand tightens on my gun.

They come, shambling out of the shadows, their flesh rotting, their eyes vacant and hungry. The undead, the scourge of this blighted world.

We form a circle, backs pressed together, weapons raised. They close in, a slow, inexorable tide of horror.

I breathe in, out, my finger curling around the trigger. Beside me, Kazuki mutters a prayer, his voice trembling. Futaba curses, her knuckles white on her knife. Hana is silent, her face set in a mask of grim determination.

The first one lunges, and I fire. The shot cracks through the air, a thunderclap of defiance. It falls, but there are more, always more.

We fight, and bleed, and scream. The forest echoes with the sounds of our struggle, a symphony of desperation and rage.

And through it all, the map burns in my pocket, a promise of salvation, a cruel jape of fate.

We will reach the fabled land. We will.

Or we will die trying, here in this godforsaken forest, just more meat for the undead to feast upon.

But even as the thought claws at my mind, I push it away. I will not let it end like this. I cannot.

For the sake of the map, and the hope it represents.

For the sake of my companions, the last shreds of my humanity.

And for myself, the man I once was, the man I could be again.

I raise my gun, and keep fighting.

The battle rages on, a relentless onslaught of gnashing teeth and grasping hands. My heart pounds in my chest, a frantic drumbeat of adrenaline and fear. I fire again and again, each shot a desperate plea for survival.

Beside me, Kazuki falls, his scream cut short by the tearing of flesh. Futaba is there in an instant, her knife flashing as she hacks at the undead, her face a mask of fury and grief.

I want to help, to save him, but there is no time. The horde is upon us, a writhing mass of decay and hunger. I can only keep shooting, keep fighting, even as my wounds bleed and my vision blurs.

And then, as suddenly as it began, it is over. The last of the undead falls, its skull shattered by Hana's precise shot. We stand there, panting, blood-soaked, alive.

But at what cost?

I look down at Kazuki's body, at the ragged wounds that mar his flesh. He was my friend, my brother in arms. And now he is gone, another victim of this endless nightmare.

The others are silent, their eyes haunted, their faces etched with pain. We have all lost so much, seen so much horror. And yet, we keep going, keep fighting, because there is no other choice.

I reach into my pocket, feel the crinkle of the map beneath my fingers. It is a slim hope, a fragile dream. But it is all we have left.

"We have to keep moving," I say, my voice raw with emotion. "We have to find this place, this sanctuary."

Futaba looks at me, her eyes hard. "And what if it's just another dead end? Another false hope?"

I meet her gaze, my own eyes burning with determination. "Then we keep searching. We keep fighting. Until we find a way out of this hell, or until we die trying."

Hana nods, her face set. "For Kazuki," she says softly.

"For Kazuki," we echo, our voices a solemn vow.

And so we press on, into the unknown, into the heart of darkness. The map leads us forward, a slender thread of hope in a world gone mad.

But even as we walk, I feel the weight of the past bearing down upon me, the ghosts of those we have lost, the sins we have committed in the name of survival.

And I wonder, not for the first time, if there can ever truly be a sanctuary for souls as damned as ours.

The map feels heavy in my hands as I carefully refold it, my fingers trembling slightly. Is this truly our salvation? Or merely another cruel trick of fate, dangling hope before us only to snatch it away?

I tuck the map back into the weathered leather pouch, the action almost reverent. It is a talisman now, a symbol of our last desperate gamble.

"We'll need to gather supplies," I say, my mind already racing ahead. "Food, water, ammunition. We don't know how long the journey will take, or what we'll face along the way."

Rei nods, her face grim. "I'll take a team to search the ruins. There may be something we can salvage."

"Be careful," I warn, my voice thick with unspoken emotion. "The undead may still linger."

She meets my gaze, her eyes haunted. "I know. We've all lost too much to carelessness."

As Rei moves off to gather her team, I turn to the others. "We'll need to fortify the camp, in case we're attacked while they're gone."

Yuuto steps forward, his young face determined. "I'll help. I'm not afraid."

I clasp his shoulder, pride mingling with sorrow. He is so young, too young for this world of blood and horror. But he has grown up fast, as we all have.

We set to work, dragging broken furniture and debris to form barricades, sharpening stakes and preparing what weapons we have left. The familiar actions are almost comforting, a grim routine we have perfected through necessity.

But even as my hands move, my mind is far away, tracing the lines of the map, imagining what lies ahead. A land without the undead, a place where we can rebuild, start anew.

It seems an impossible dream, a fantasy born of desperation. But what choice do we have? To stay here is to die, slowly consumed by the relentless tide of the undead.

At least this way, we have a chance. A slim chance, perhaps, but a chance nonetheless.

And so we prepare, our hearts heavy with the weight of the unknown, our souls scarred by the horrors we have endured. But beneath it all, a flicker of hope, fragile and stubborn, refusing to be extinguished.

For hope is all we have left in this shattered world, and we will cling to it with all the strength we possess, even as the darkness closes in around us.

The sun dips below the horizon, painting the sky in hues of blood and fire. It's a fitting omen for the journey ahead, a reminder of the hell we are about to embark upon.

We gather around the flickering campfire, our faces etched with shadows and unspoken fears. Maikoru stands, the map clutched tightly in his hands, his eyes gleaming with a feverish intensity.

"We leave at dawn," he says, his voice low and resolute. "We travel light, take only what we need. We move fast, stay alert. The undead will be watching, waiting for any sign of weakness."

Nods of assent ripple through the group, a silent acknowledgment of the risks we are about to take. We have all seen the horrors that lurk beyond the safety of our camp, the shambling corpses with their rotting flesh and insatiable hunger.

But we have also seen the toll that this existence has taken on us, the slow erosion of our humanity, the gnawing despair that eats away at our souls. We are living on borrowed time, and we know it.

As the night wears on, I find myself drawn to the edge of the camp, staring out into the darkness. The jungle looms before me, a tangle of shadows and hidden dangers, and I feel a shiver run down my spine.

What lies ahead? What horrors will we face on this desperate quest for salvation? The questions gnaw at me, but I push them aside. There is no turning back now, no room for doubt or hesitation.

We have made our choice, and we will see it through, no matter the cost. For in this world of the undead, there are only two options: survive or perish.

And I, for one, am not ready to give up just yet.

The flames danced before my eyes, casting flickering shadows across my weathered face. Ghosts of the past swirled in the smoke, their whispers a haunting chorus in my mind. How long had I carried these sins, these burdens that etched themselves into my very soul?

My thoughts drifted, as they often did, to a distant time when innocence still clung to me like a shroud. I saw my father, the great chief, his shoulders stooped under the weight of our people's lives.

"Maikoru, my son," he said, his voice a rumble in the night. "To lead is to sacrifice. To protect is to bear the scars of many."

I watched as he pored over maps by candlelight, strategizing, planning, always vigilant. The lines on his face deepened with each passing day, the toll of leadership carving itself into his features.

"But father," I asked, my child's voice small in the darkness, "what of our family? What of the life we might have had?"

He turned to me then, his eyes holding a sorrow I was too young to comprehend. "We are the shield, Maikoru. We stand between our people and the horrors that would consume them. It is our duty, our burden to bear."

And bear it he did, until the very end. I saw the sacrifices he made, the pieces of himself he left behind with each battle, each decision that shaped the fate of our tribe.

The memories shifted, blurring together like ink on parchment. Faces, places, moments lost to the relentless march of time. But always, the weight remained, the knowledge that I too must carry the mantle of leadership, the sins of my father now mine to bear.

The fire crackled, embers rising into the night sky like lost souls seeking redemption. But for me, redemption seemed a distant dream, forever out of reach. The ghosts of my past lingered, their accusations a constant companion in the shadows of my mind.

And then, the memory of that fateful day surfaced, as vivid as the flames before me. The day I first encountered the undead, the day my world shattered like fragile glass.

I was barely a man, still clinging to the vestiges of my youth, when the abomination stumbled into our village. Its flesh hung in rotting strips, its eyes vacant and hungry. The stench of death clung to it like a shroud, permeating the air with its foulness.

Fear gripped me, a primal terror that rooted me to the spot. I watched, paralyzed, as the creature lurched forward, its gnarled hands reaching for the nearest victim. Screams filled the air, the sound of my own heartbeat thundering in my ears.

"Run, Maikoru!" someone shouted, their voice distant and muffled. But I couldn't move, couldn't tear my gaze away from the horror before me. It was as if the undead thing had reached into my very soul, its corruption seeping into the marrow of my bones.

And then, a blur of movement, a flash of steel. My father, the chief, stood before the monster, his sword raised in defiance. He fought with a fierce determination, his blade slicing through decaying flesh and brittle bone. But even as he struck the killing blow, I saw the toll it took on him, the way his shoulders sagged beneath the weight of his duty.

That was the first of many encounters, each one leaving its mark upon my psyche. The undead became a constant presence, a nightmare from which there was no waking. And with each battle, each horrendous face that leered at me in the darkness, I felt a piece of myself slip away, lost to the abyss of my own fear.

But it was Akiko's fate that truly shattered me, the guilt of my failure consuming me like a ravenous beast. She was the light in my darkness, the one pure thing in a world of decay and despair. And I couldn't save her.

I remember the moment she turned, her once gentle eyes clouding with a feral hunger. The woman I loved, the mother of my child, reduced to a soulless husk. And I, her husband, her protector, could only watch in helpless agony as she succumbed to the undead curse.

"Forgive me, my love," I whispered, my voice breaking with the weight of my anguish. "I failed you. I failed our family."

The questions haunted me, tormenting my every waking moment. Could I have done more? Was there some way, some path I hadn't seen? The burden of leadership, the mantle passed down from my father, seemed to mock me in my grief. What good was power, if I couldn't even protect those I held most dear?

I closed my eyes, the memories threatening to engulf me. The campfire burned low, the night pressing in around me like a suffocating cloak. And still, the ghosts of my past lingered, their whispers a constant reminder of my sins, my failures.

How long I sat there, lost in the labyrinth of my own torment, I couldn't say. But as the first light of dawn began to creep over the horizon, I felt a hand on my shoulder, a familiar presence at my side.

"Maikoru," Riku's voice cut through the haze of my thoughts, his tone gentle yet firm. "You're not alone in this. You never were."

I turned to face my oldest friend, the one who had stood by me through every trial and hardship. In his eyes, I saw a reflection of my own pain, a shared understanding of the burdens we carried.

"I remember the day we first met," Riku continued, settling down beside me. "We were just boys then, full of dreams and innocence.

We'd sneak off to the river, pretending we were great warriors, fighting imaginary battles."

A ghost of a smile tugged at my lips, the memories of those carefree days a bittersweet ache in my chest. "We were going to change the world," I murmured, my voice rough with emotion. "Make it a better place."

Riku nodded, his gaze distant. "But the world had other plans. The undead came, and everything changed."

I sensed the shift in his tone, the weight of his own demons pressing down upon him. "You've never talked about what happened," I said softly, "to your family."

Riku's jaw clenched, his eyes glistening with unshed tears. "It was my younger sister, Hana," he began, his voice barely above a whisper. "She was bitten, infected. I... I couldn't save her."

The anguish in his words mirrored my own, a shared pain that bound us together. "I watched her turn, watched the light fade from her eyes. And I knew, in that moment, that I would do anything to protect our people, to spare them from that same fate."

I placed a hand on Riku's shoulder, a silent gesture of support. "We've both lost so much," I said, my voice heavy with the weight of our shared grief. "But we can't let it define us, can't let it consume us."

Riku met my gaze, a flicker of determination sparking in his eyes. "You're right. We have to keep fighting, for the sake of our tribe, for the memory of those we've lost."

As the sun rose over the horizon, casting its golden light across the barren landscape, I felt a renewed sense of purpose, a flicker of hope amidst the darkness. With Riku by my side, I knew we could face whatever horrors lay ahead, that we could carry on, even in the face of our own demons.

The day was already proving to be a trial, the scorching sun beating down upon us as we made our way through the desolate streets. Riku, ever vigilant, scanned our surroundings with a practiced eye, his katana at the ready.

"There," he whispered, pointing towards a dilapidated building. "Movement in the shadows."

I followed his gaze, my heart pounding in my chest as I caught sight of the undead, their rotting flesh hanging in tatters from their bones. They shambled forward, their hollow eyes filled with an insatiable hunger.

Riku sprang into action, his blade flashing in the sunlight as he cleaved through the nearest zombie with a sickening crunch. I marveled at his skill, the way he moved with a fluid grace, dispatching the undead with a grim efficiency.

But even Riku's prowess couldn't keep them at bay forever. They swarmed us, their grasping hands clawing at our flesh, their fetid breath hot against our skin. I felt the icy grip of fear take hold, my mind clouding with panic.

It was then that Riku's quick thinking saved us. "The building," he shouted, gesturing towards a narrow window. "We can bottleneck them, take them out one by one."

I followed his lead, scrambling through the opening and into the musty interior. Riku took up position at the window, his blade a blur of motion as he cut down the undead that tried to force their way inside.

"We can't keep this up forever," I panted, my lungs burning with exertion. "We need a way out."

Riku's eyes darted around the room, searching for an escape. "There," he said, pointing to a rickety staircase. "It should lead to the roof. We can make our way across, find a way down on the other side."

We fought our way to the stairs, the undead hot on our heels. I could feel their fingertips brushing against my back, the stench of decay overwhelming. But we pressed on, fueled by desperation and the unrelenting will to survive.

As we emerged onto the roof, the sun's glare nearly blinded me. I squinted against the light, my eyes adjusting to the sight of the city stretched out before us, a wasteland of crumbling buildings and abandoned streets.

"We'll make it through this," Riku said, his voice filled with a quiet determination. "We'll find a way to end this nightmare, to build a future without the undead."

I looked at him then, saw the unwavering belief in his eyes. And I knew, with a certainty that settled deep in my bones, that I would follow him to the ends of the earth, that I would fight by his side until my last breath.

"A future," I echoed, the word tasting strange on my tongue, a concept almost forgotten in this world of constant horror. "It seems like an impossible dream."

Riku shook his head, a small smile tugging at the corners of his mouth. "Not impossible. Just waiting for us to make it a reality." He looked out over the city, his gaze distant. "We'll find a way, Maikoru. We'll build a world our fallen would be proud of."

As we stood there, the wind whipping at our clothes, the moans of the undead rising from the streets below, I felt a flicker of something I hadn't experienced in a long time: hope. It was a fragile thing, a delicate flame in the darkness, but it was there, burning steadily in my chest.

And with Riku by my side, I knew we would keep that flame alive, no matter what horrors the world had in store for us. Together, we would fight, we would endure, we would find a way to make that impossible dream a reality.

The flickering flames of the campfire cast dancing shadows across Riku's face as we sat together, our minds lost in the labyrinth of memories. The weight of our shared past hung heavy in the air, a tangible presence that bound us together more tightly than the bonds of blood.

"Do you remember," Riku began, his voice barely audible above the crackling of the fire, "the day we first met? We were just kids then, so full of dreams and hopes for the future."

I nodded, a faint smile tugging at the corners of my lips. "I remember. We were going to change the world, you and I. We were going to be heroes."

Riku chuckled, a sound that seemed to belong to a different time, a different life. "We were naive back then, weren't we? We had no idea what true heroism meant."

"No," I agreed, my gaze drifting to the dark shadows that lurked beyond the firelight. "We didn't. But we learned, didn't we? Through blood and pain and loss, we learned what it means to fight for something greater than ourselves."

Riku was silent for a long moment, his eyes distant and haunted. "I never would have survived this long without you, Maikoru," he said at last, his voice thick with emotion. "You've been my rock, my anchor in this sea of madness. I don't know how to thank you for that."

I reached out and clasped his shoulder, feeling the solid strength beneath my fingers. "You don't need to thank me, Riku. You've been there for me just as much as I've been there for you. We're in this together, until the end."

Riku met my gaze, his eyes shining with a fierce determination that I knew mirrored my own. "Until the end," he repeated, his words a solemn vow.

We sat there for a long time, lost in our own thoughts, the weight of our past and the uncertainty of our future pressing down upon us like a physical force. But even in the midst of that darkness, I felt a glimmer of something like hope, a faint flicker of light that refused to be extinguished.

As long as Riku was by my side, I knew we would keep fighting, keep pushing forward, no matter how bleak the road ahead might seem. Together, we would find a way to build a better world, a world where the undead were nothing more than a distant memory, and the dreams we had once held so dear could finally become a reality.

Riku's voice cut through the silence, his words like a blade forged in the fires of our shared purpose. "We'll find that place, Maikoru. That land without the undead. I swear it on my life. I'll stand by your side, protect our tribe, until we reach that promised sanctuary or die trying."

His declaration hung in the air between us, a tangible thing, heavy with the weight of our commitment. I turned to face him fully, searching his eyes for any trace of doubt or hesitation, but found only an unwavering resolve that burned brighter than the dying embers of our campfire.

In that moment, I realized that Riku was more than just my friend, more than just my loyal companion. He was my anchor, my beacon in the darkness, the one person who truly understood the depth of my pain and the magnitude of my burden.

I reached out and pulled him into a fierce embrace, feeling the warmth of his body seep into my own, chasing away the chill that had settled deep in my bones. We clung to each other like two drowning men, our love for each other and our shared purpose the only things keeping us afloat in this sea of despair.

As we held each other, I felt a sudden surge of emotion, a tidal wave of gratitude and affection that threatened to overwhelm me. Tears pricked at the corners of my eyes, but I blinked them away, refusing to let them fall.

We have a long road ahead of us, I thought, my mind already racing with the challenges that lay before us. The undead hordes, the treacherous landscapes, the constant threat of death and decay that dogged our every step.

But even as those dark thoughts swirled through my mind, I felt a flicker of something else, a glimmer of hope that refused to be extinguished. With Riku by my side, I knew we could face whatever trials lay ahead, that we could carve out a new future for ourselves and our tribe, no matter how daunting the odds might seem.

And so we held each other, our love and our shared purpose shining through the darkness like a beacon, guiding us forward into an uncertain future. The road ahead would be long and fraught with peril, but together, we would find a way to prevail, to build a better world from the ashes of the old.

The dense rainforest closed in around us as we trudged through the underbrush. My boots squelched in the moist earth with each labored step, an unrelenting rhythm that echoed the pounding of my guilt-ridden heart. Osamu's death weighed heavily upon my shoulders, a burden I was unworthy to bear.

I led our ragged band of survivors but felt like an impostor. How could I protect them when I had failed my own brother? The faces of those who depended on me - Riku, Akiko, Hiro, Kenji - their trusting eyes bore into my back as I forged ahead.

My grip tightened on the makeshift spear, the roughly hewn wood biting into my calloused palm. Eyes darted from shadow to shadow, seeking out the undead horrors that lurked just out of sight. The eerie stillness made the hair on my nape prickle.

"Maybe we should turn back," Akiko whispered, her voice quavering.

I didn't respond. Couldn't respond. Indecision gnawed at my insides like a starving rat. Sweat trickled down my brow, stinging my eyes. I blinked it away.

"Maikoru? What should we-" Riku started.

"Quiet!" I hissed. "Stay alert."

My tone was harsher than intended. Riku fell silent, hurt flickering across his face. Regret twisted my gut but I pushed it down. I had to stay strong. Had to keep moving forward.

But to where? To what end? These questions tormented me as we delved deeper into the verdant hell, further from any chance of salvation. The stench of rot and despair hung heavy in the humid air.

I was drowning in doubt, in fear, in sorrow. Each step took me closer to an abyss from which there was no return. The ghosts of my failures dogged my heels, their skeletal fingers clawing at my resolve.

I didn't know if I had the strength to go on. But I had no choice. Their lives depended on me. Even as my own soul crumbled to ash, I would lead them. I had to. For Osamu.

A twig snapped.

We froze, hearts pounding, ears straining. Silence thrummed like a plucked string drawn taut. My hand tightened on my machete's worn grip, knuckles white.

"What was-" Yumi's tremulous question died in her throat as an unearthly moan shattered the stillness. A chorus of groans and snarls followed, rising in volume, in hunger.

They emerged from the foliage like a nightmare made flesh. Rotting faces contorted in mindless fury, yellowed teeth gnashing, milky eyes filled with insatiable bloodlust. Dozens of them. Too many.

"Run!" I roared. "To the clearing!"

Panic exploded. The group bolted, crashing through the underbrush, heedless of the branches that tore at clothes and skin. I brought up the rear, slashing at grasping hands, decaying fingers. The stink of putrefaction clogged my nostrils.

Riku stumbled ahead of me, nearly pitching face-first into the dirt. I hauled him up by his collar and shoved him forward. "Don't stop! Keep going!"

My lungs seared. My heart jackhammered against my ribs. The undead surged after us, an implacable tide of gnashing teeth and flailing limbs. Their rasping growls dogged our steps, drowning out the pounding of blood in my ears.

We burst into the clearing and whirled to face our pursuers, chests heaving. They lurched from the treeline, some crawling, others loping with unnatural speed. Driven by an endless hunger that could never be sated.

I raised my machete, the blade catching the wan light. Desperation clawed at my throat. We were cornered. Trapped.

This was it. This was how it ended. In a godforsaken jungle, torn to shreds by ravenous corpses. All my efforts, all my promises - for nothing.

Osamu's face swam before me, pale and still in death. I had failed him. Failed them all. Grief and despair crashed over me, threatening to drag me under.

But I couldn't surrender. Not yet. I met Riku's terrified gaze, saw my own hopelessness reflected back at me. Akiko and Yumi huddled behind us, clutching each other, sobbing.

I swallowed past the aching lump in my throat. Drew in a shuddering breath. And charged.

The machete cleaved through fetid flesh and brittle bone, spraying ichor. I hacked and slashed with reckless abandon, pouring all my anguish, all my fury into each blow. Faces I once knew leered back at me, their features contorted into soulless masks. Former friends. Neighbors. All reduced to mindless, ravenous shells.

I fought like a man possessed, spinning and pivoting, my blade a whirling dervish of destruction. But for every one I cut down, two more surged forward to take its place. An endless sea of grasping hands and snapping jaws.

My arms burned with fatigue. My lungs screamed for air. The world narrowed to the frenzied crush of bodies, the coppery stench of gore.

Then Riku was beside me, his sword flashing crimson. "I've got your back," he panted, his shoulder pressed against mine.

A hysterical laugh bubbled up my throat. In that moment, I loved him fiercely, this brave, foolish boy who stood with me against certain death.

Together, we battled on, holding the horde at bay. Buying precious seconds for Akiko and Yumi to escape. But it was a losing fight, and we both knew it.

The zombies pressed closer, their rotting fingers snagging at our clothes, our hair. I felt my strength waning, my swings growing sluggish. Despair settled over me like a shroud.

I had always known it would end this way. That my sins would catch up with me in the end. That I could never outrun the ghosts of my past.

I closed my eyes, waiting for the inevitable agony of teeth sinking into flesh. Of being dragged down and ripped apart.

Praying that oblivion would claim me swiftly. That I would finally find the peace that had eluded me for so long.

Then the world exploded in a blaze of light and heat, and everything went black.

My eyes fluttered open to chaos, my head throbbing. Smoke choked the air, stinging my lungs. All around, zombies staggered and flailed, their moans rising to a fever pitch.

I struggled to my feet, disoriented. Riku materialized at my side, his face smeared with grime. "What happened?" I croaked.

He shook his head, just as bewildered. "I don't know. Some kind of explosion."

Across the clearing, I spotted Akiko and Yumi, huddled behind a fallen tree. They were alive. We were all still alive, against impossible odds.

But the reprieve was short-lived. Already, the zombies were recovering, turning their hungry gazes back in our direction. We had to move, now, or be overrun.

I grabbed Riku's arm, hauling him towards the others. "Fall back!" I yelled, my voice ragged. "Into the trees!"

We ran, crashing through the undergrowth, thorns tearing at our skin. Behind us, the horde gave chase, their snarls echoing through the forest.

My lungs burned, my muscles screamed in protest. But I pushed on, fueled by raw terror, by the primal need to survive.

Branches whipped my face, drawing blood. My foot caught on a root, sending me sprawling. Riku hauled me up, half-dragging me along.

"Keep going," he urged, his breath coming in ragged gasps. "Don't look back."

But I couldn't help it. I glanced over my shoulder, into the faces of our pursuers. Into the faces of the damned.

And in that moment, I saw him. Osamu, his once kind eyes now milky and soulless. His slack mouth dripping with gore.

A wail built in my throat, a keening of pure anguish. The grief hit me like a physical blow, driving me to my knees.

I wanted to lay down, to let the horde take me. To join Osamu in oblivion, where I belonged.

But Riku wouldn't let me. He seized my shoulders, shaking me roughly. "Maikoru, snap out of it!" he shouted, his voice edged with panic. "We need you! I need you!"

I looked at him through a veil of tears, this boy who had become my brother. And I knew I couldn't abandon him, couldn't abandon any of them.

With a shuddering breath, I pushed myself to my feet. Locked away the grief, the guilt, the searing pain.

There would be time enough for that later, if we survived. For now, I had to be strong. For them, if not for myself.

"Let's go," I said, and together we ran on, deeper into the darkness, with the dead snapping at our heels.

Just as the horde closed in, the ground beneath our feet shuddered. A deafening boom split the air, and the night exploded in a blaze of light and heat.

I hit the ground hard, ears ringing, vision swimming. Around me, the others sprawled in the dirt, stunned and disoriented.

But the zombies... the zombies were scattered. Blown back by the force of the blast, their rotting bodies smashed against the trees.

For a moment, I could only blink stupidly, my grief-fogged mind struggling to comprehend what had happened. Then Riku let out a whoop of joy.

"We're saved!" he cried, scrambling to his feet. "Maikoru, look!"

I followed his gaze, and through the smoke, I saw them. Figures emerging from the shadows, armed to the teeth. Living, breathing humans.

Relief crashed over me, so intense it was almost painful. We weren't alone. We weren't doomed. Not yet, anyway.

But as the newcomers approached, wariness crept in alongside the relief. We'd learned the hard way that not all survivors were friendly.

I pushed myself up, ignoring the protest of bruised muscles. Stepped forward to meet them, one hand resting on the hilt of my knife.

"Who are you?" I demanded, my voice rough with smoke and unshed tears.

The leader, a grizzled man with a scar bisecting his face, met my gaze unflinchingly. "We're the ones who just saved your sorry hides," he growled. "A little gratitude wouldn't go amiss."

I bristled at his tone, but Riku intervened before I could retort. "We are grateful," he said quickly. "More than you know. I'm Riku, and this is Maikoru. We've been on our own for... a long time."

Something flickered in the man's good eye. Understanding, perhaps. Or maybe just pity.

"Jiro," he said at last, extending a hand. "Looks like we got here just in time."

I hesitated, torn between suspicion and desperation. We needed allies, needed safety in numbers. But trust was a luxury we could ill afford.

In the end, though, what choice did we have? We were battered, bone-weary, heartsick. We couldn't go on alone.

I reached out, clasped Jiro's hand in a brief, firm shake. A pact sealed in blood and ash.

"Thank you," I said, the words tasting strange on my tongue. "We owe you our lives."

Jiro shrugged. "We're all in this together," he said. "Come on. Let's get out of here before those bastards get back up."

As if on cue, a moan rose from the fallen zombies. A twitching hand, an ankle rotating at an impossible angle.

We didn't need to be told twice. Hurriedly, we gathered our few belongings and fell into step behind Jiro.

I brought up the rear, my katana drawn and ready. But even as I scanned the shadows for danger, my thoughts were turned inward.

To Osamu, lost forever. To the fragile new bond forged in desperation. To the long road ahead, shrouded in uncertainty.

We had survived the night. But in this brutal new world, survival was a fleeting thing.

All we could do was keep moving forward. One step at a time, into the waiting dark.

The weight of leadership bore down on me as we trudged through the undergrowth, a ragtag band of survivors thrown together by fate and misfortune. Jiro and his companions, Akiko and Kenji, moved with a quiet efficiency born of long practice. They knew this terrain, knew how to navigate its perils.

I envied their certainty, their sense of purpose. My own path seemed shrouded in doubt and regret.

Riku fell into step beside me, her presence a silent comfort. She alone understood the depth of my grief, the scars that Osamu's death had left upon my soul.

"We'll make it through this," she said softly, her hand brushing mine in a fleeting touch. "We have to."

I wanted to believe her, wanted to cling to that fragile hope. But hope was a dangerous thing in this world, as treacherous as the zombies that lurked in every shadow.

We walked on in silence, the only sound the rustling of leaves beneath our feet and the distant cries of unknown beasts. The forest seemed to close in around us, a living, breathing entity that watched our every move with malevolent intent.

"We'll rest here," Jiro said at last, gesturing to a small clearing. "Take turns on watch. We'll move on at first light."

I sank to the ground, my body aching with exhaustion. But even as I closed my eyes, I knew that sleep would bring no respite.

The ghosts of the past haunted me, their whispers a constant reminder of all that I had lost. All that I had failed to protect.

And yet, as I looked around at the faces of my companions, old and new, I felt a flicker of something like hope. A sense that perhaps, just perhaps, we might find a way through this darkness.

Together.

I sat alone in a dimly lit corner of our makeshift camp, my face buried in my hands, my body trembling with despair. The weight of it all pressed down on me, threatening to crush my very soul. How had it come to this? The responsibility I carried felt like an anchor dragging me into an abyss of hopelessness.

My thoughts swirled in a tempest of anguish. The faces of the fallen, those we had lost along the way, haunted me. Their blood stained my hands, invisible yet indelible. I had failed them, failed to protect them from the horrors that stalked us relentlessly. Each decision I made, each path I chose, seemed to lead only to more suffering and death.

In the suffocating silence, the ghosts of my sins whispered their accusations. They taunted me, reminding me of my inadequacy, my weakness. How could I possibly lead our people to safety when I could barely hold myself together? The fabled land we sought felt like a cruel mirage, forever out of reach, taunting us with false hope.

I lifted my head, my eyes scanning the shadows that danced across the crumbling walls. The makeshift camp felt more like a tomb than a refuge. The air was thick with the stench of decay and despair. We were nothing more than walking corpses, clinging to a fragile existence in a world that had long since forsaken us.

My gaze fell upon the huddled forms of the survivors, their faces etched with the same weariness and despair that consumed me. They looked to me for guidance, for strength, but I had none left to give. I was a hollow shell, a mere echo of the leader I once aspired to be.

The weight of their lives, their hopes and dreams, pressed down on my shoulders, threatening to shatter me. How could I bear this burden alone? The responsibility was a noose around my neck, tightening with each passing moment. I longed for relief, for an escape from this waking nightmare.

Yet even in the depths of my despair, a flicker of something else stirred within me. A faint glimmer of... what? Hope? Love? It was a feeling I hardly recognized anymore, buried beneath layers of guilt and self-loathing. But there it was, like a distant light in the darkness, calling me back from the brink.

I closed my eyes, trying to grasp onto that fleeting sensation. Images of Riku flashed through my mind - her gentle smile, her unwavering strength, the love that shone in her eyes even in our darkest moments. She was my anchor, my reason to keep going when all seemed lost.

But even as I clung to thoughts of her, doubt crept in like a poisonous vine. Did I deserve her love? Did I deserve anyone's trust or loyalty? I had led them into this hell, and now I struggled to find a way out. The weight of my failures pressed down on me, threatening to crush what little hope remained.

In that moment, sitting alone in the shadows, I felt the full weight of my despair. It was a living thing, clawing at my insides, whispering doubts and fears that I couldn't shake. The responsibility I carried was a burden too heavy to bear, and yet I knew I had no choice but to keep going, to find a way forward for the sake of those who relied on me.

But in that dark corner of our makeshift camp, with only my thoughts for company, I couldn't help but wonder... was there any hope left for us at all? Or were we merely delaying the inevitable, marching towards a fate worse than death itself? The questions haunted me, even as I struggled to find the strength to rise and face another day in this unforgiving world.

As I sat there, lost in the depths of my own despair, a gentle hand settled on my shoulder. I looked up, my vision blurred by unshed tears, and found Riku kneeling beside me. Her eyes, once bright with hope and determination, now shimmered with concern and a love so profound it stole my breath.

"Maikoru," she whispered, her voice a soothing balm to my wounded soul. "You can't give up. Not now, not ever."

I shook my head, the weight of my failures too heavy to bear. "I've led them to their deaths, Riku. I've failed them all."

But Riku refused to accept my words. She cupped my face in her hands, forcing me to meet her gaze. "You haven't failed anyone. You've given them hope, a reason to keep fighting even when all seems lost."

Her words, spoken with such conviction, began to chip away at the walls of despair that had engulfed me. I searched her face, desperate for a lifeline, for something to cling to in this sea of hopelessness.

"Our people need you, Maikoru. They need your strength, your courage, your unwavering determination to lead them to safety." Riku's voice grew stronger, filled with a passion that ignited a spark within me.

"And I need you. I need the man I fell in love with, the man who never backs down from a challenge, no matter how daunting it may seem."

She leaned in closer, her forehead pressing against mine, and in that moment, I felt the power of our bond, the strength that flowed between us. It was a force that could not be broken, a love that transcended the horrors of this world.

"Together, we can overcome anything," Riku whispered, her breath warm against my skin. "Our love is the light that will guide us through this darkness, the beacon that will lead our people to the promised land."

As I listened to her words, I felt something stir within me, a flicker of hope that had been all but extinguished. Riku's love, her unwavering faith in me, was a balm to my battered soul, a reminder that even in the darkest of times, there was still something worth fighting for.

Her words, like a lifeline thrown to a drowning man, pulled me from the depths of my despair. I clung to them, allowing their warmth to seep into my bones, chasing away the chill of hopelessness that had settled there.

"Do you remember the night we first met?" Riku asked softly, a hint of a smile playing at the corners of her lips. "How we danced beneath the stars, our bodies moving as one, as if we'd known each other for lifetimes?"

I nodded, the memory flooding back to me in a rush of bittersweet nostalgia. It seemed like a lifetime ago, a different world entirely, one untouched by the horrors that now plagued our every waking moment.

"That night, I knew I'd found something special in you," Riku continued, her voice barely above a whisper. "A connection that could never be broken, a love that would endure through any trial or tribulation."

She reached up, her fingers gently tracing the contours of my face, wiping away the tears that I hadn't even realized I'd shed. "And when you stood before our people, rallying them with your words, your conviction, I knew I'd fallen for a man destined for greatness."

I leaned into her touch, my eyes fluttering closed as I savored the sensation of her skin against mine. In that moment, I felt a glimmer of something I'd thought long lost: hope.

"You've always seen the best in me, even when I couldn't see it myself," I murmured, my voice hoarse with emotion. "Your love, your belief in me... it's the only thing that's kept me going in this godforsaken world."

Riku smiled then, a radiant, heart-stopping smile that seemed to chase away the shadows that had taken root in my soul. "And it always will, my love. No matter what lies ahead, we'll face it together. Our love will be the light that guides us home."

As Riku's words washed over me, I felt the weight of my doubts and fears begin to lift, replaced by a growing sense of purpose and determination. The shadows that had plagued my mind for so long seemed to recede, driven back by the sheer force of her love and unwavering faith in me.

But even as I drew strength from her presence, I couldn't help but wrestle with the lingering ghosts of my past. The lives I'd taken, the choices I'd made... they haunted me still, whispering their accusations in the darkest corners of my mind.

I pulled away from Riku's embrace, my gaze falling to the ground as I struggled to find the words to express the turmoil within me. "I'm not the man you think I am," I said at last, my voice barely more than a whisper. "I've done things, terrible things... things that can never be forgiven."

Riku's hand found mine, her fingers intertwining with my own as she pulled me back to her. "We've all done things we regret," she said softly, her eyes searching mine. "But that doesn't define who we are. It's what we do now, in this moment, that matters."

As I looked into her eyes, I saw a reflection of my own soul - broken, battered, but not defeated. And in that moment, I felt something shift within me, a subtle but profound change that seemed to illuminate the darkest recesses of my being.

The doubts and fears that had once consumed me began to fall away, replaced by a growing sense of clarity and purpose. I realized then that Riku's love wasn't just a comfort in the face of adversity - it was a source of strength, a guiding light that could lead me out of the darkness and into a brighter future.

With a newfound sense of resolve, I straightened my shoulders and met Riku's gaze, my eyes blazing with a fire that had long been extinguished. "You're right," I said, my voice steady and strong. "We can't change the past, but we can fight for a better tomorrow. And with you by my side, I know we can overcome anything."

My hand found Riku's, our fingers intertwining as if they were always meant to be joined. The warmth of her touch spread through me, a silent reminder of the unbreakable bond we shared. In that moment, I felt a surge of emotion so powerful it threatened to overwhelm me.

As I gazed into her eyes, I saw a reflection of my own love, a love that had endured through the darkest of times and the most harrowing of trials. It was a love that had been forged in the fires of adversity, tempered by the weight of our shared experiences and the depth of our understanding.

And as I lost myself in the depths of her eyes, I found myself marveling at the power of that love. It was a force that could move mountains, a light that could pierce the darkest of nights. It was a love that could inspire hope in the face of despair, courage in the face of fear, and strength in the face of weakness.

I realized then that our love was more than just a bond between two people - it was a testament to the resilience of the human spirit, a symbol of the indomitable will that had carried us through the apocalypse and beyond.

And as I held Riku's hand in mine, I knew that no matter what challenges lay ahead, no matter how insurmountable the odds may seem, our love would be the anchor that kept us grounded, the compass that guided us home.

For in a world where death and destruction reigned supreme, where the very fabric of society had been torn asunder, our love was the one constant that remained, the one thing that could never be taken from us.

And with that knowledge, I felt a renewed sense of purpose, a burning desire to keep fighting, to keep pushing forward, no matter the cost. For with Riku by my side, I knew that anything was possible, that even in the darkest of times, there was still hope for a brighter tomorrow.

I made a silent vow, a solemn promise to myself and to Riku, that I would not rest until our people were safe, until we had reached the fabled land that promised salvation. No matter the challenges that lay ahead, no matter the horrors that we may face, I would not falter, I would not yield.

For too long, I had allowed my own doubts and fears to consume me, to hold me back from doing what needed to be done. But no more. With Riku's love as my guiding light, I would find the strength to lead our people through the darkness, to forge a path to a better future.

And so, with a deep breath and a newfound sense of determination, I rose to my feet, pulling Riku up with me. Our eyes met, and in that moment, I saw the same fierce resolve that burned within my own heart reflected back at me.

Together, we would face whatever awaited us on this path to salvation, our love the armor that would shield us from the horrors of this world, our bond the weapon that would strike down any foe that dared stand in our way.

As we stepped forward, out into the unknown, I felt a sense of hope blossoming within my chest, a fragile yet powerful thing that had long been absent from my life. And though the road ahead was sure to be fraught with peril, I knew that with Riku by my side, there was nothing we could not overcome.

For in the end, it was not the destination that mattered, but the journey itself - a journey of love, of hope, and of the unbreakable human spirit that refused to be extinguished, even in the face of the apocalypse itself.

The dying fire flickers, casting haunting shadows across the walls of my makeshift shelter. In the wavering light, I glimpse my own tormented face, eyes hollow with self-doubt. Have I led them astray? Am I worthy to guide them through this accursed wasteland?

My hands tremble as I grasp the tattered journal, its pages heavy with the names of the fallen. So many lost under my command. Each one a scar upon my soul, a reminder of my failures as a leader. Tears blur the ink, smudging their memory. But I cannot let myself forget. Cannot allow their sacrifices to be in vain.

I trace my finger down the list of the dead, each name an accusation. Yumi, fierce warrior, felled by gnashing teeth as I watched helplessly. Hiro, loyal friend, devoured before my eyes when I hesitated a fatal instant. Kaori, bright spirit, extinguished by my indecision, my inability to act.

The journal slips from my grasp and thuds to the dirt floor. Dust motes swirl in the firelight as I clench my fists, digging nails into flesh. The pain is a welcome distraction from the agony in my heart. How can I continue on, knowing it was my choices, my frailties that sealed their doom? What right do I have to lead, when all I leave behind me is a trail of corpses?

The fire gutters and wanes, plunging my refuge into darkness. I make no move to feed the fading flames. The shadows welcome me like a shroud, cloaking me in my despair. As I sink into black rumination, the ghosts of my fallen comrades rise up to haunt me, just as they do each eternal night...

I spring to my feet, unable to endure the accusing specters a moment longer. Pacing like a caged beast, I stalk the confines of the shelter, my steps heavy and leaden. Each footfall resounds with the weight of my guilt, the burden of my failures.

"I should have been faster, stronger, wiser," I mutter, my voice a hoarse rasp in the oppressive silence. "If only I had seen the signs, anticipated the horde's movements. If only I had been a better leader, a better protector..."

My mind reels, replaying the horrific events that stole the lives of my tribesmen. The surprise attack that caught us unawares, the relentless tide of undead that overwhelmed our defenses. I see Yumi, surrounded and fighting valiantly to her last breath. Hiro, dragged down by grasping hands as he pushed me to safety. Kaori, her scream cut short as she vanished beneath a writhing mass of decay.

"Forgive me," I whisper, my plea falling on deaf ears. "I failed you all. I should have been the one to fall, not you."

I halt my pacing, my chest heaving with the force of my self-recrimination. The weight of my failures threatens to crush me, to drive me to my knees. But I cannot succumb, cannot let their deaths be for naught.

"I will do better, be better," I vow, my voice trembling with the intensity of my resolve. "I will lead our people to the promised land, or die trying. Your sacrifices will not be in vain."

The words feel hollow, a paltry offering to the memory of the fallen. But they are all I have, all I can cling to in the face of the unrelenting darkness. I must find the strength to go on, to shoulder the burden of leadership, no matter the cost to my soul.

With a shuddering breath, I turn back to the dying embers of the fire, stoking the feeble flames to life once more. The flickering light casts shifting shadows on the walls, a grim reminder of the specters that haunt me. But I will not let them consume me, will not let despair claim me.

For the sake of the living, for the sake of those who still depend on me, I will endure. I will lead. Even if it damns me in the end.

The faces of the fallen haunt me, their accusing gazes boring into my soul. I see them in every shadow, hear their whispers in the silence of the night. They come to me in flashes, vivid and unrelenting, a constant reminder of my failures.

Akira, his eyes wide with terror as the horde descended upon him. Yumi, her scream cut short by the gnashing teeth of the undead. And little Hiro, his small hand slipping from mine as I fled, leaving him to a fate worse than death.

Their blood stains my hands, their names forever etched into my memory. I should have been faster, stronger, smarter. I should have found a way to save them all. But I was weak, and they paid the price for my inadequacy.

The weight of their loss bears down on me, a suffocating burden that threatens to crush me beneath its unyielding mass. I sink to my knees, my body wracked with sobs that tear at my throat, my chest heaving with the force of my anguish.

"I'm sorry," I choke out, the words a pitiful offering to the spirits of the dead. "I'm so sorry."

But apologies are meaningless in the face of such profound loss, and the echoes of my own voice mock me in the stillness of the night. The despair rises within me, a black tide that threatens to pull me under, to drown me in the depths of my own self-loathing.

I curl in on myself, my forehead pressed to the cold, unyielding ground, my fingers clawing at the dirt as if seeking absolution. But there is no forgiveness to be found, no redemption for the sins of the past.

The faces of the fallen continue to swirl before my eyes, their voices a discordant chorus of condemnation. I am lost, adrift in a sea of my own making, with no hope of finding my way back to shore.

And yet, even as the darkness threatens to consume me, a small, stubborn spark of defiance flickers to life within my chest. I cannot let their deaths be in vain. I cannot let despair claim me, not when there are still those who depend on me.

With trembling fingers, I clutch at my chest, my heart aching beneath the weight of responsibility. The burden of leadership, once a source of pride, now feels like a millstone around my neck, dragging me down into the depths of self-doubt.

"Can I truly keep them safe?" I whisper, my voice a ragged whisper in the stillness of the night. "Am I capable of leading them through this nightmare?"

The question hangs in the air, unanswered, as the flickering flames of the dying fire cast dancing shadows on the walls of my makeshift shelter. The faces of the living and the dead alike seem to watch me, their eyes filled with a silent accusation.

A memory rises unbidden, a ghost from a past I would rather forget. The decision had seemed so clear at the time, a choice between the lesser of two evils. But now, with the benefit of hindsight, I see the true cost of my actions.

The village had been overrun, the infected swarming through the streets like a plague of locusts. We had barricaded ourselves in the town hall, a desperate last stand against the hordes of the undead. But our supplies were running low, and the moans of the infected grew louder with each passing hour.

"We have to make a break for it," I had said, my voice trembling with a false bravado. "It's our only chance."

But not everyone had agreed. Some had wanted to wait, to hold out hope for a rescue that might never come. And in the end, it had fallen to me to make the call.

"We go," I had said, my heart heavy with the weight of the decision. "Now, while we still can."

And so we had fled, abandoning the relative safety of the town hall for the chaos of the streets. But in the end, it had been for nothing. The infected had been waiting for us, their numbers too great to overcome.

I had watched as they fell, one by one, their screams echoing in my ears as they were torn apart by the ravenous horde. And I had run, my legs pumping with a desperate energy, my lungs burning with each gasping breath.

But even as I ran, I knew that I had failed them. That their blood was on my hands, their deaths a stain on my soul that could never be washed clean.

And now, as I sit in the darkness of my shelter, the weight of that failure threatens to crush me. The faces of the dead stare back at me, their eyes filled with a silent accusation.

"I'm sorry," I whisper, my voice a broken rasp. "I'm so sorry."

But the words feel hollow, a futile gesture in the face of such profound loss. And as the night wears on, I am left alone with my guilt, a solitary figure haunted by the ghosts of his past mistakes.

The fire fades to embers, casting a sickly orange glow across the room. I stare into the dying flames, my mind a whirlwind of conflicting thoughts and emotions.

I know that I must lead my people to safety, that their lives depend on my strength and guidance. But the fear gnaws at me, a constant companion that whispers its doubts in the silence of the night.

What if I am not strong enough? What if I make the wrong choice, and doom us all to a fate worse than death?

The weight of responsibility bears down on me, a crushing burden that threatens to steal the very breath from my lungs. I can feel it pressing against my chest, a physical ache that grows with each passing moment.

And then, without warning, my legs give out beneath me. I collapse to the ground, my body shaking with a violent tremor that I cannot control.

Sobs wrack my frame, tears streaming down my face as I finally give voice to the anguish that has been building inside me. The guilt, the shame, the overwhelming sense of helplessness - it all comes pouring out in a torrent of raw emotion.

I pound my fists against the unyielding earth, my knuckles splitting and bleeding with the force of my blows. But the pain is a welcome distraction from the agony that tears at my heart.

"I can't do this," I choke out, my words barely audible over the sound of my own ragged breathing. "I'm not strong enough. I'm going to fail them, just like I failed the others."

The admission hangs in the air, a damning indictment of my own weakness. And as I lie there, my body spent and my spirit broken, I am forced to confront the terrible truth that I have tried so hard to deny.

I am not the leader they need. I am just a man, flawed and fallible, struggling to find his way in a world gone mad. And in that moment, I am certain of only one thing.

Amidst the depths of my despair, a faint shimmer of light pierced the darkness—a memory of Riku's unwavering faith in me. Her voice echoed through the chambers of my tortured mind, a soothing balm upon my scarred soul. "You are our leader, Maikoru," she had said, her eyes shining with a fierce belief. "You will guide us through this forsaken world, to a haven where we may find peace."

I clung to her words like a drowning man grasping for driftwood in a raging sea. With trembling fingers, I brushed away the tears that stained my weathered cheeks. A newfound determination flickered to life within me, a fragile flame amidst the suffocating shadows. I would not let Riku's faith be in vain. I would rise from the ashes of my guilt and lead my people onward, through the bleak wasteland that stretched before us.

The fabled land called to me, a distant promise of redemption. It whispered of a place where the weight of my sins might finally be lifted, where the ghosts of those I failed could find rest. I would carry their memory with each step, a solemn vow to honor their sacrifice. For in their names, I would press forward, battling the horrors that lurked in the shadows, until we reached that mythical sanctuary or perished in the attempt.

With a shuddering breath, I pushed myself to my feet, my body aching with the weariness of a thousand lifetimes. The path ahead was shrouded in uncertainty, a winding trail through a landscape of nightmares. But I would not falter. I would be the beacon of hope my people needed, the unyielding shield against the relentless tide of death. For in this shattered world, hope was the only currency that mattered, and I would spend it freely to keep my flock alive.

I stood tall, my shoulders squared, gathering the tattered remnants of my strength. The weight of leadership settled upon me like a cloak of thorns, each barb a reminder of the lives that depended on my every decision. I could feel their eyes upon me, searching for guidance, for the unwavering resolve that would lead them through the bleak wastes of this ruined world.

"We press on," I declared, my voice raw with emotion. "We honor the fallen by enduring, by clawing our way towards the promise of sanctuary. It is in their memory that we fight, that we defy the grasping hands of death."

I cast my gaze across the haggard faces of my companions, their features etched with the scars of unimaginable horrors. In their eyes, I saw the flicker of hope, a desperate yearning for a future beyond the constant struggle for survival. It was a fragile thing, easily snuffed out by the relentless darkness that surrounded us, but I would nurture it with every fiber of my being.

For a fleeting moment, I allowed myself to remember those we had lost, their faces forever etched into the depths of my soul. Their sacrifices weighed heavily upon me, a burden I would carry until my final breath. But in their memory, I found the strength to persevere, to lead my people through the twisted labyrinth of this apocalyptic nightmare.

"We will not let their deaths be in vain," I whispered, my words a solemn vow. "We will find the fabled land, and there we will build a new life, one where the ghosts of our past can finally find peace."

With a final, resolute nod, I turned towards the horizon, my gaze fixed upon the unknown path that stretched before us. Each step was a battle against the insidious whispers of doubt, against the chilling embrace of despair. But I would not yield, for I had made a promise to the fallen, to the living, and to myself.

And so, with a heavy heart and an unyielding spirit, I led my people onward, towards the distant glimmer of hope that beckoned us from beyond the veil of darkness. The road ahead was fraught with peril, but together, we would face the challenges that lay in wait, united by the bonds of survival and the unbreakable ties of our shared humanity.

In the desolate wasteland of the apocalypse, we would find our way, or we would perish trying. For in the end, it was all we could do to honor the memory of those who had gone before us, and to forge a path towards a future where hope could once again take root in the barren soil of our shattered world.

As I stepped forward, the weight of my past sins clung to me like a tattered shroud, threatening to drag me back into the depths of despair. The faces of the fallen haunted my every waking moment, their accusing eyes boring into my soul, demanding retribution for my failures. But I could not allow myself to be consumed by the darkness within, for the lives of those who remained depended upon my strength, my resolve.

With each passing day, the journey grew more arduous, the threats more dire. The undead hordes lurked in every shadow, their hunger insatiable, their numbers ever-growing. And yet, we persevered, driven by the unyielding determination to survive, to find a place where we could once again call home.

As the sun dipped below the horizon, painting the sky in hues of crimson and gold, I found myself lost in thought, haunted by the memories of all that we had lost. The sacrifices we had made weighed heavily upon my heart, a constant reminder of the price we had paid for our survival. But even in the midst of such sorrow, I clung to the faint glimmer of hope that flickered within my chest, a testament to the indomitable spirit of humanity.

And so, I pressed onward, my footsteps echoing through the desolate landscape, a solitary figure against the backdrop of a world gone mad. The path ahead was shrouded in uncertainty, but I knew that I could not falter, could not succumb to the temptation of surrender. For in the end, it was the promise of a better tomorrow that drove me forward, the belief that someday, we would find a place where the horrors of the past could be laid to rest, and a new chapter could begin.

With a deep breath, I steeled myself against the trials that lay ahead, my gaze fixed upon the horizon, my heart filled with a grim determination. And as I stepped into the unknown, I knew that whatever darkness awaited me, I would meet it head-on, armed with the strength of my convictions and the unwavering support of those who stood beside me. For in this world of chaos and despair, it was the bonds of love and loyalty that would see us through, guiding us towards the light that beckoned from beyond the shadows.

The survivors huddled together, their hollow eyes gazing at me with a fragile glimmer of hope. Riku stood beside me, her hand a gentle pressure at the small of my back, lending me strength. I breathed deep, summoning the words that might reignite the fire within their broken spirits.

"Look around you," I said, my voice echoing in the stillness. "See the faces of those who have fought, those who have lost, those who have endured." My gaze swept over them, taking in the scars, the haunted expressions, the weariness etched into every line. "We have seen horrors that no living soul should witness. We have faced death, again and again, and yet here we stand."

A murmur rippled through the crowd, a rustling of agreement tinged with sorrow. I could feel their pain, their despair, as if it were a tangible thing, pressing down upon us all. But I knew that within them, buried beneath the layers of suffering, lay a resilience that refused to be extinguished.

"Remember those we have lost," I continued, my voice growing stronger, more insistent. "Remember their sacrifice, their courage in the face of unimaginable darkness." Images flashed through my mind—faces of fallen comrades, friends, family. Their ghosts lingered, whispering in the shadows, a constant reminder of the price we had paid. "Their memory lives on in each of us, fueling our determination to survive, to find a way out of this nightmare."

I paused, letting the weight of my words settle upon them. In the silence, I could hear the ragged breaths, the muffled sobs, the quiet sniffles of those who fought to hold back their tears. Riku's hand tightened on my back, a silent reassurance, a reminder that I was not alone in this struggle.

"We have come so far," I said, my voice dropping to a whisper that somehow carried across the gathered survivors. "Through the blood and the terror, the loss and the despair, we have clung to each other, to the hope that someday, somehow, we might find a way to live again." I closed my eyes, feeling the ache in my chest, the heaviness that never quite left. "And though that hope may seem fragile, though the path ahead may be shrouded in darkness, we must not falter."

A single sob broke the silence, followed by another, and another. Tears flowed freely now, the weight of grief and trauma finding release in the stillness of the moment. I, too, felt the sting of tears behind my eyes, the ache of loss that never quite faded, no matter how many days passed.

I drew in a deep breath, steadying myself against the swell of emotion that threatened to overwhelm me. When I spoke again, my voice was stronger, infused with a spark of determination that flickered to life within me. "There is a place, a land spoken of in whispers, where the undead do not tread. A place where we might rebuild, where we might reclaim the lives that were stolen from us."

I could see the flicker of hope in their eyes, the desperate longing for a world beyond the horrors we had endured. It was a fragile thing, that hope, so easily snuffed out by the relentless cruelty of this new reality. But I clung to it, nurtured it, fanned its flames with every word I spoke.

"In this land, we can start anew. We can build homes, plant crops, raise our children without fear of the undead's hunger. We can create a community, a sanctuary, a place where we might remember what it means to truly live." The words flowed from me, painting a picture of a future that seemed almost too good to be true. But I believed in it, with every fiber of my being. I had to believe, for the sake of those who looked to me for guidance, for hope.

Riku's presence beside me was a steadying force, a reminder of the love and loyalty that had sustained me through the darkest of times. I drew strength from her, from the unwavering support that radiated from her like a beacon in the night.

"It will not be an easy journey," I cautioned, my voice dropping to a somber tone. "The path ahead is fraught with danger, with challenges we can scarcely imagine. But we have faced the unimaginable before, and we have survived. Together, we can overcome anything that stands in our way."

I looked out over the sea of faces, seeing the flicker of determination that began to take hold, the spark of hope that refused to be extinguished. They were a ragged bunch, scarred and weary, but there was a strength in them, a resilience that had carried them through the end of the world.

"We will find this land," I vowed, my voice ringing with conviction. "We will carve out a new life, a new future, from the ashes of the old. And though the memories of those we have lost will forever haunt us, we will honor them by living, by fighting, by refusing to let the darkness claim us."

A murmur of assent rippled through the gathered survivors, a quiet but powerful declaration of their resolve. I felt the weight of their trust, their faith in me, settling upon my shoulders like a mantle. It was a burden I would gladly bear, a responsibility I would not shirk.

For in that moment, as I stood before them, I knew that our fate lay not in the hands of the undead, but in our own. We would forge our own path, write our own story, and though the pages might be stained with blood and tears, they would be ours, and ours alone.

I met each of their gazes, one by one, seeing the flicker of fear, the shadow of doubt that lingered in their eyes. It was a fear I knew all too well, a doubt that had gnawed at my own soul in the darkest hours of the night. But I also saw something else, a glimmer of defiance, a spark of courage that refused to be extinguished.

"I know you're afraid," I said softly, my voice barely above a whisper. "I know you've seen horrors that no one should ever have to witness, endured losses that have torn your hearts asunder. But we cannot let that fear consume us, cannot let it rob us of our hope, our humanity."

I stepped forward, my gaze sweeping over the assembled survivors, willing them to feel the strength of my conviction, the depth of my belief in them. "We are stronger than we know," I declared, my words ringing out in the stillness of the night. "We have survived this far, not by chance, but by the force of our will, the power of our unity. And it is that same strength, that same resilience, that will carry us through the trials to come."

I saw the change come over them then, saw the way their shoulders straightened, their eyes brightened with a newfound resolve. It was as if a weight had been lifted from their souls, a burden shared and lessened by the knowledge that they were not alone, that they had each other to lean on, to draw strength from.

And in that moment, I felt a flicker of something I had not dared to feel in a long time: hope. Hope that we could find a way through this nightmare, hope that there was still a future worth fighting for, a life beyond the constant struggle for survival.

It was a fragile thing, that hope, a delicate flame that could be snuffed out by the slightest breath of despair. But as I looked out at the faces of the survivors, saw the determination etched upon their features, I knew that we would nurture that flame, would shelter it against the darkness that sought to engulf us.

For in the end, it was all we had left, that flickering light of hope, that stubborn refusal to surrender to the night. And though the road ahead would be long and treacherous, though the ghosts of our past would forever haunt our steps, we would walk it together, bound by the unbreakable bonds of our shared humanity.

I cleared my throat, my voice raw with emotion as I spoke once more. "Each of you, every single one, carries within you the strength to face the horrors that lie ahead. It is a strength born of the trials you have endured, the losses you have suffered. It is a strength that cannot be broken, cannot be taken from you."

I paused, letting my words sink in, watching as the survivors straightened their shoulders, a flicker of defiance in their eyes. "Find that strength now, that inner warrior that has carried you this far. Embrace it, let it fuel your every step, your every breath. For it is only together, only as one, that we can hope to survive, to forge a path through the darkness."

The survivors exchanged glances, a silent communication passing between them. I could see the uncertainty in some, the hesitation born of countless disappointments, of hopes dashed upon the unforgiving rocks of reality. But there was something else there too, a glimmer of resolve, a spark of determination that refused to be extinguished.

It was Riku who stepped forward first, his hand clasping mine, his eyes blazing with a fierce intensity. "We stand with you, Maikoru. To the end, whatever that may be."

One by one, the others followed suit, their voices rising in a chorus of agreement, their hands joining ours in a symbol of unity, of unbreakable solidarity. And as I looked out at their faces, saw the resolve etched upon their features, I felt a surge of pride, of gratitude for the unwavering loyalty they had shown me, for the trust they had placed in my hands.

But beneath that pride lurked a darker emotion, a gnawing guilt that tore at my insides. For I knew the truth, knew the secret that I had kept hidden from them all, the secret that threatened to tear apart everything we had built.

It was a truth that haunted my every waking moment, a specter that lurked in the shadows of my mind, whispering its poison into my ears. And though I tried to push it aside, tried to focus on the task at hand, I could feel its presence, could feel the weight of my sins pressing down upon me like a physical force.

For in the end, I was no hero, no savior to be venerated and followed. I was a liar, a deceiver, a man whose past was steeped in blood and betrayal. And though I longed to confess, to lay bare the truth and beg for their forgiveness, I knew that I could not, knew that the price of honesty was too high to pay.

And so I pushed down the guilt, forced a smile to my lips as I rallied the survivors once more, my voice ringing out with a confidence I did not feel. "Together, we will face the darkness. Together, we will find a way through. This, I promise you."

But even as the words left my mouth, I could feel the hollowness behind them, could taste the bitter tang of deceit upon my tongue. And as we set about our preparations, as we readied ourselves for the trials to come, I could only pray that my sins would not be the undoing of us all, that the ghosts of my past would not rise up to claim us in the end.

The preparations were a flurry of activity, a desperate scramble to gather what meager supplies we had left. I watched as the survivors moved about the camp, their faces etched with a grim determination that belied the fear lurking just beneath the surface.

And yet, even as they worked, I could feel their eyes upon me, could sense the unspoken questions that lingered in the air between us. They looked to me for guidance, for strength, for the promise of a future that seemed increasingly out of reach.

I did my best to reassure them, to offer words of encouragement and hope, but the words felt hollow in my mouth, like ashes upon my tongue. For how could I offer them comfort when I myself was haunted by the ghosts of my own past?

As I moved through the camp, I caught sight of Riku, her eyes meeting mine across the sea of weary faces. In that moment, I saw the trust that shone in her gaze, the unwavering faith that she had placed in me. And it was like a knife to my heart, a reminder of all that I stood to lose if the truth of my past ever came to light.

I forced myself to look away, to focus on the task at hand. There would be time enough for regrets later, when the dead were no longer snapping at our heels. For now, all that mattered was survival, the desperate fight to keep the darkness at bay.

But even as I threw myself into the preparations, I could feel the weight of my secrets bearing down upon me, could feel the icy tendrils of fear wrapping themselves around my heart. And I knew that sooner or later, the truth would come out, that the sins of my past would finally catch up with me.

And when that day came, I could only pray that the survivors would find it in their hearts to forgive me, to understand the choices I had made in the name of survival. For in the end, we were all just pawns in this game of life and death, all just struggling to find our way in a world gone mad.

My hands trembled as I helped distribute supplies among the survivors, my mind still reeling from the oath we had just taken. The words echoed in my ears, a solemn promise to stand together, to fight for a better future no matter the cost. But even as I moved among them, offering words of encouragement and support, I could feel the weight of my own hypocrisy bearing down upon me.

For how could I ask them to trust me, to put their lives in my hands, when I myself was hiding a secret that could tear us all apart? The memories came unbidden, flashes of a life I had tried so hard to forget. The choices I had made, the blood on my hands...

I shook my head, trying to banish the thoughts from my mind. There would be time enough for self-recrimination later, when we were safe and the dead were nothing more than a distant nightmare. For now, I had to focus on the task at hand, on ensuring that we had everything we needed to survive the journey ahead.

"Maikoru, we're running low on medical supplies," Riku said softly, appearing at my side with a worried frown. "I'm not sure we have enough to last us more than a few days."

I nodded grimly, my mind already racing with possibilities. "We'll have to make do with what we have," I said, my voice low and urgent. "And pray that we don't run into any more trouble along the way."

But even as the words left my lips, I knew that trouble was always waiting just around the corner, that in this world of the undead, no one was ever truly safe. And as I watched the survivors disperse to their assigned tasks, each one filled with a new sense of purpose and determination, I could only hope that I would be strong enough to lead them through the darkness ahead.

For in the end, that was all I could do - hope and pray and fight with every ounce of strength I had left. And maybe, just maybe, if I could keep them alive long enough, if I could get them to the fabled land that promised safety and a new beginning, then perhaps I could finally find a way to atone for my sins and start anew.

But until then, I would have to bear the weight of my secrets alone, would have to live with the knowledge that at any moment, the truth could come spilling out and destroy everything we had fought so hard to build. It was a heavy burden to bear, but one that I knew I had no choice but to shoulder.

For in this world of the undead, trust was a fragile thing, and once broken, it could never be fully mended again.

I felt Riku's hand tighten around mine, her slender fingers intertwining with my calloused ones. In that brief moment of respite, I drew strength from her presence, from the warmth of her skin against my own. Our eyes met, and in that silent exchange, I saw the same fierce determination that burned within my own soul.

We had been through so much together, Riku and I. She had seen me at my lowest points, had watched me struggle with the demons that haunted my every waking moment. And yet, she had never once wavered in her support, had never once questioned my ability to lead our people to safety.

It was a trust that I knew I did not deserve, a faith that I feared I would one day betray. For there were secrets that I kept buried deep within my heart, sins that I had committed in the name of survival. And if Riku ever discovered the truth about my past, about the things I had done...

I shuddered at the thought, my hand tightening involuntarily around hers. She looked at me then, her brow furrowing in concern. "Maikoru, what is it?" she asked, her voice barely more than a whisper.

I forced a smile to my lips, shaking my head slightly. "It's nothing," I lied, the words tasting bitter on my tongue. "Just... promise me that you'll stay by my side, no matter what happens."

Riku's eyes softened, and she lifted her free hand to cup my cheek. "Always," she murmured, her thumb brushing lightly over my skin. "I will never leave you, Maikoru. Not in this life, or the next."

I leaned into her touch, my eyes drifting closed for a moment as I savored the feeling of her skin against mine. It was a small comfort, but one that I clung to like a drowning man to a life raft.

For in that moment, with Riku by my side and the weight of my secrets bearing down upon me, I knew with a grim certainty that the road ahead would be long and treacherous. And as much as I wanted to believe in the promise of a brighter future, I could not shake the feeling that lurked in the darkest

As the chapter drew to a close, I watched as the survivors scattered to their various tasks, their movements infused with a newfound sense of purpose. The air hummed with a palpable energy, a stark contrast to the oppressive despair that had hung over us for so long.

I moved through the camp like a wraith, my steps measured and deliberate as I surveyed the preparations. Everywhere I looked, I saw the fruits of my labors - the spark of hope that I had kindled in their hearts, the determination that now burned bright in their eyes.

But even as I walked among them, I could not shake the sense of unease that coiled like a serpent in the pit of my stomach. It was a feeling I knew all too well, the same one that had haunted me since the day the world had ended.

I paused beside a group of survivors who were sorting through a pile of scavenged supplies, their hands moving with a feverish intensity. One of them looked up as I approached, a young woman with haunted eyes and a face lined with grief.

"Do you really think we can make it?" she asked, her voice trembling slightly. "To the fabled land, I mean."

I met her gaze, my own eyes hooded and inscrutable. "We have to," I replied, my voice low and measured. "There is no other choice."

The woman nodded, her lips pressing together in a thin line. "I just... I can't help but wonder what we'll find when we get there. If it even exists at all."

I placed a hand on her shoulder, my fingers digging into the worn fabric of her shirt. "It exists," I said, my voice taking on a strange, almost hypnotic quality. "And when we find it, all of our struggles will have been worth it. Trust in that, if nothing else."

The woman looked at me for a long moment, her eyes searching mine for some sign of deception. But I had become a master at hiding the truth, even from myself.

As I walked away, I could feel the weight of my secrets pressing down upon me, threatening to crush me beneath their burden. But I pushed them aside, focusing instead on the task at hand.

For I knew that the journey ahead would test us all, in ways we could scarcely imagine. And if we were to have any hope of surviving, we would need to be strong - stronger than we had ever been before.

The thought sent a shiver down my spine, and I quickened my pace, my mind already racing ahead to the challenges that lay before us. But even as I walked, I could not escape the feeling that something was watching me from the shadows, waiting for the perfect moment to strike.

The narrow path twisted like a serpent through the desolate wasteland. Sharp outcroppings threatened to impale us with every step. I glanced over at Riku, his eyes darting left and right, probing the shadows for horrors yet unseen. We walked in lockstep, warriors bound by blood and battle.

"How much further?" rasped a voice behind me. Akiko, the widow. Her husband's blood still stained her shirt.

"As far as it takes," I replied without turning. My eyes never left the path ahead. In this forsaken world, a moment's inattention could spell doom for us all.

The survivors trudged onward, a motley band of the damned. Innocent no longer. Not after the atrocities we'd witnessed...and committed. Each of us bore the weight of our sins like a leaden shroud. There could be no forgiveness. Not anymore.

Rounding a jagged bend, our steps faltered. The path ended at a sheer cliff that plunged into nothingness below. A strangled gasp echoed from the group. Riku glanced my way and arched an eyebrow.

Approaching the precipice, I surveyed our predicament. The abyss yawned wide, promising a quick death to any who dared its depths. But we had not come this far to surrender now. Fate would not claim us yet.

"Ropes and ladders," I said, my voice steady despite the unease churning in my gut. "We scale down."

Worried murmurs rippled through the survivors. I turned to face them, my gaze hard as flint.

"Unless you prefer to sit and rot under this blighted sun. Your choice."

One by one, their eyes met mine—haunted, defiant, resolved. Koji, the grizzled hunter, stepped forward with coils of weathered rope. The others rummaged for branches to fashion into makeshift rungs.

As they worked, I gazed out over the yawning chasm. Far below, a distant rumble echoed up the cliff face, raising the hairs on my nape. Riku touched my shoulder, his fingers digging deep.

"You hear it too," he said. Statement of fact, not a question.

I nodded once, slowly. That sound portended only one thing in this bleak hellscape. The Dead were nigh...and they hungered.

We began our treacherous descent, the ropes biting into our flesh as we lowered ourselves down the sheer rock face. The air grew thick with tension, each ragged breath a countdown to the inevitable. I took the lead, my senses honed to a razor's edge, searching for any sign of the horde.

Riku followed close behind, his presence a steadying force in the face of the unknown. I could feel his eyes boring into my back, a silent promise that he would stand by my side until the bitter end.

As we reached the bottom of the cliff, the growls intensified, a chorus of hunger and decay that sent shivers down my spine. I scanned the dense thicket that stretched before us, the tangled vegetation offering a thousand hiding places for the undead.

"Stay close," I whispered, my voice barely audible above the pounding of my own heart. "And keep your weapons ready."

I plunged into the undergrowth, machete in hand, every sense attuned to the slightest movement or sound. The survivors followed, their fear palpable in the air. We moved as one, a fragile lifeline in a world gone mad.

The thicket seemed to close in around us, the twisted branches grasping at our clothes like skeletal fingers. I pushed forward, my mind racing with the knowledge that each step brought us closer to the waiting horde.

Riku's voice drifted through the gloom, low and urgent. "Maikoru, I don't like this. It's too quiet."

I nodded, my grip tightening on the machete. The silence hung heavy, broken only by the distant groans of the undead. It was the calm before the storm, the held breath before the plunge.

Suddenly, a twig snapped beneath my foot, the sound as loud as a gunshot in the stillness. I froze, my heart hammering against my ribs. The growls intensified, a rising tide of hunger and rage.

They were coming.

A rotting hand shot out from the undergrowth, its decaying fingers clawing at my face. I reacted on instinct, dodging the attack with a swift sidestep. My machete flashed in the dappled light, a silver arc of retribution. The blade connected with the zombie's neck, severing head from body in a single, brutal stroke.

The creature crumpled to the ground, but there was no time for triumph. More zombies emerged from the thicket, their moans and snarls filling the air like a hellish chorus. They came at us from all sides, a writhing mass of putrid flesh and gnashing teeth.

Riku was at my side in an instant, his sword a blur of motion. We fought together, our movements fluid and precise, born of countless battles and a bond forged in blood. The undead fell before us, our blades finding their marks with deadly efficiency.

But even as we cut them down, more took their place. The horde seemed endless, a nightmare made flesh. I felt the weight of exhaustion pulling at my limbs, the toll of countless sleepless nights and endless days of running.

"There's too many!" Riku shouted, his voice raw with desperation.

I knew he was right. We were being overwhelmed, the sheer number of zombies threatening to drag us down into oblivion. But I couldn't let it end like this. Not after all we'd sacrificed, all we'd lost.

I reached deep within myself, summoning the last reserves of strength. The faces of the fallen flashed before my eyes, the weight of their memory a crushing burden. I would not let their deaths be in vain.

With a primal roar, I surged forward, my machete a whirlwind of destruction. I carved a path through the horde, my body moving on instinct, fueled by a desperate, unyielding will to survive.

Riku fought beside me, his sword singing a song of death. Together, we pushed back against the tide of undead, our blades flashing in the dying light. The ground grew slick with blood and viscera, the air heavy with the stench of decay.

But even as we fought, I knew it was only a matter of time. The horde was relentless, their numbers seeming to multiply with each passing moment. My arms burned with fatigue, my lungs screaming for air.

And then, just as I felt the last of my strength ebbing away, I heard a sound that made my blood run cold. A low, guttural growl, deeper and more menacing than anything I'd heard before.

I turned, my heart seized with a new kind of terror. There, emerging from the depths of the thicket, was a zombie unlike any I'd ever seen. It was massive, its body a twisted mass of bulging muscle and rotting flesh. Its eyes blazed with a feral, inhuman intelligence.

The creature fixed its gaze on me, and in that moment, I knew I was staring into the face of death itself.

I stood frozen, paralyzed by the sheer enormity of the creature before me. Its massive frame towered over the other zombies, its grotesque features twisted into a snarl of pure, unadulterated hunger.

"Maikoru!" Riku's voice cut through the haze of my terror. "We have to fall back, regroup with the others!"

But I couldn't move, couldn't tear my eyes away from the monstrosity that now dominated the battlefield. It took a step forward, the ground quaking beneath its feet.

"Maikoru, please!" Riku's desperate plea finally broke through my stupor. I shook myself, forcing my leaden limbs into action.

We fought our way back to the others, the massive zombie's roars echoing in our ears. The survivors huddled together, their faces etched with the same fear that gripped my own heart.

"What do we do?" someone whispered, their voice trembling.

I looked around at their faces, these people who had trusted me to lead them to safety. The weight of their lives pressed down on me, threatening to crush me beneath its burden.

But I couldn't let them see my fear, couldn't let them know the depths of my own despair. I straightened my shoulders, forcing a confidence I didn't feel into my voice.

"We stand together," I said, my words ringing out across the clearing. "We fight as one, and we do not falter. This is our moment, our chance to prove that we are stronger than the darkness that seeks to consume us."

I saw the flicker of hope in their eyes, the way their grips tightened on their weapons. And in that moment, I knew that even if we fell, even if the horde claimed us all, we would go down fighting, our spirits unbroken.

We turned to face the oncoming tide of death, our hearts pounding in unison. The massive zombie let out a roar that shook the very foundations of the earth, and then it charged, its monstrous form barreling towards us with terrifying speed.

I raised my machete, the weight of it familiar and comforting in my hand. Beside me, Riku let out a battle cry, his sword flashing in the fading light.

And together, we ran forward to meet our fate, the last remnants of humanity standing tall in the face of the apocalypse.

As the massive zombie bore down upon us, I felt a strange sense of calm settle over me. The world seemed to slow, each heartbeat stretching into an eternity. I could see every detail with startling clarity - the rotting flesh peeling from the creature's face, the madness swirling in its milky eyes, the gaping maw lined with jagged teeth.

I sidestepped its initial lunge, my machete flashing out to carve a deep gash across its chest. Black ichor sprayed from the wound, splattering my face and arms, but I barely noticed. All that mattered was the dance, the deadly choreography of survival.

Riku was a blur of motion at my side, his sword a silvery arc of destruction. He moved with a grace that belied his exhaustion, each strike precise and lethal. Together, we drove the behemoth back, our blades finding the gaps in its defenses, our movements perfectly synchronized.

But even as we fought, I could feel the weight of my sins bearing down upon me. The faces of those I had failed, those I had been forced to leave behind, swam before my eyes. Their accusations echoed in my mind, a chorus of the damned that threatened to drag me down into the depths of despair.

"Stay focused!" Riku shouted, his voice cutting through the haze of my guilt. "We can't afford to lose you, not now!"

I shook my head, trying to clear the cobwebs from my mind. He was right. I couldn't let the past consume me, not when the future of our people hung in the balance.

With a roar of defiance, I launched myself at the zombie, my machete aimed at its skull. The blade sank deep, cracking bone and severing the connection between brain and body. The creature staggered, its movements growing sluggish and uncoordinated.

But even as it fell, I could see more zombies emerging from the treeline, their numbers seeming to grow with every passing second. They shambled forward, a tide of rotting flesh and gnashing teeth, their hunger insatiable.

I turned to Riku, my eyes wide with a fear I could no longer hide. "There's too many," I whispered, my voice hoarse with desperation. "We can't hold them all off."

He met my gaze, his own eyes filled with a grim determination. "Then we go down fighting," he said, his hand finding mine and squeezing tight. "Together, until the very end."

I nodded, a strange sense of peace settling over me. If this was to be our final stand, then so be it. We would face the horde as one, our spirits united in defiance of the darkness.

And so, with a final battle cry, we charged forward into the sea of undeath, our hearts filled with the knowledge that even in death, we would never be alone.

The zombies closed in, their rotting hands grasping at our flesh, their fetid breath hot against our skin. I moved on instinct, my machete a blur of silver as it sliced through the air, severing limbs and splitting skulls. Beside me, Riku fought with a savage grace, his own blade carving a path of destruction through the horde.

"Maikoru!" he shouted over the din of battle. "We need to push through to the other side!"

I nodded, my breath coming in ragged gasps as I hacked and slashed my way forward. The zombies seemed endless, their numbers replenishing as quickly as we could cut them down. But still, we fought on, driven by a desperate need to survive.

As we neared the center of the horde, a massive zombie emerged from the throng, its bloated body towering over the others. Its eyes glowed with a malevolent intelligence, and it let out a roar that shook the earth beneath our feet.

"That one's mine," I growled, my grip tightening on my machete.

Riku glanced at me, his eyes narrowing. "Maikoru, don't be a fool. We take it together, or not at all."

I hesitated, torn between my desire for vengeance and the knowledge that he was right. But before I could respond, the zombie lunged forward, its massive fists swinging with deadly force.

We dove to either side, rolling to our feet and circling the creature like wolves around a wounded elk. It turned to face us, its movements slow but powerful, each step shaking the ground.

I darted in, my machete flashing in the dim light. The blade bit into the zombie's flesh, but it seemed to barely notice the wound. It swung at me, its fist grazing my shoulder and sending me stumbling backward.

Riku leaped forward, his own blade carving a deep gash across the creature's chest. It roared in pain and rage, its arms flailing wildly. One massive hand caught Riku across the face, sending him flying backward into the horde.

"Riku!" I screamed, my heart seizing with fear. But there was no time to check on him, not with the giant zombie bearing down on me.

I dodged another blow, my machete striking sparks against the creature's rotting flesh. It lunged forward, its jaws snapping at my face. I twisted away, my blade slicing through the air and burying itself deep in the zombie's eye socket.

The creature let out a final, agonized roar before collapsing to the ground, its massive body twitching and convulsing. I staggered back, my chest heaving with exertion, my eyes scanning the horde for any sign of Riku.

And there he was, his blade flashing in the darkness as he fought his way back to my side. His face was bruised and bloodied, but his eyes burned with the same fierce determination I knew so well.

"Thought you could leave me behind, did you?" he asked, his voice rough with exertion.

I shook my head, a smile tugging at the corners of my lips. "Never," I said. "We started this together, and that's how we'll finish it."

And with that, we turned to face the remaining zombies, our blades held high, our hearts beating as one. The end might be near, but we would face it together, bound by a love that even death could not sever.

The battle raged on, the stench of death and decay filling my nostrils, the screams of the dying echoing in my ears. My blade was slick with blood, my arms aching from the strain of endless combat. But still, I fought on, driven by a desperate need to survive, to protect those who looked to me for leadership.

Beside me, Riku was a whirlwind of destruction, his sword cutting through the horde like a scythe through wheat. His face was a mask of grim determination, his eyes blazing with a fire that even the undead could not extinguish.

And then, finally, it was over. The last zombie fell, its lifeless body hitting the ground with a sickening thud. The survivors stood amidst the carnage, panting and covered in blood, their faces etched with exhaustion and triumph.

I turned to Riku, my heart swelling with gratitude and affection. He met my gaze, his lips curving into a weary smile. In that moment, I knew that our bond was stronger than ever, forged in the crucible of battle and tempered by the unbreakable ties of love.

"We did it," I said, my voice hoarse with emotion. "We survived."

Riku nodded, his hand finding mine and squeezing it tightly. "We always do," he said. "No matter what the world throws at us, we'll face it together."

I turned to the survivors, my voice ringing out across the battlefield. "You have all shown incredible bravery and resilience today," I said. "You have overcome the greatest challenge yet, and proved that even in the darkest of times, hope and humanity can still prevail."

The survivors cheered, their voices rising in a chorus of joy and relief. And as I looked out over the sea of faces, I knew that we had taken another step towards our ultimate goal - a world where the living could thrive once more, free from the shadow of the undead.

But even as I basked in the glow of victory, I couldn't shake the feeling that our journey was far from over. The road ahead would be long and treacherous, filled with dangers both known and unknown. And yet, with Riku by my side and the strength of the survivors at my back, I knew that we would face whatever challenges lay ahead with courage and determination.

For in this world of death and despair, love and hope were the only things worth fighting for. And I would fight for them until my last breath, no matter the cost.

My lungs burned as I gulped in the stale, blood-tinged air. The weight of the battle hung heavy on my shoulders, but a flicker of hope danced in my chest. We had survived. We had won.

Riku's hand gripped my shoulder, his touch a silent reassurance. Our eyes met, a wordless exchange of the horrors we had witnessed and the unbreakable bond forged in the crucible of combat.

I surveyed the survivors, their faces etched with a tapestry of exhaustion and relief. They clung to each other, desperate for the comfort of human connection in a world where death reigned supreme.

"We did it," I said, my voice hoarse from shouting orders and battle cries. "We've proven that we are stronger than the undead. That we will not be broken."

The survivors nodded, a flicker of determination sparking in their haunted eyes. They knew, as I did, that this was but one battle in an endless war. The promised land beckoned, a siren's call that drew us ever onward.

As we gathered our meager belongings and prepared to continue our journey, a sense of resilience settled over the group. We had stared into the abyss and emerged victorious, our spirits tempered by the fires of adversity.

"Riku, take point," I said, my gaze sweeping the horizon for any signs of danger. "We press on, no matter what lies ahead."

He nodded, his jaw set with grim determination. Together, we led the survivors forward, our footsteps echoing through the desolate landscape. The ghosts of our past sins whispered in our ears, a constant reminder of the price we had paid for survival.

But even as the darkness closed in around us, I clung to the faint glimmer of hope that flickered in my heart. We were one step closer to our goal, one step closer to rebuilding the world we had lost.

And though the road ahead was shrouded in uncertainty, I knew that we would face it together, united by the bonds of survival and the unshakable belief that even in the darkest of times, light could still be found.

As we emerged from the suffocating grasp of the rainforest, my eyes squinted against the harsh glare of the sun-scorched desert stretching before us like a baked corpse. The lifeless valley, devoid of the undead horrors, filled me with a fleeting sense of relief. Had we finally outrun our demons, both living and deceased? Or was it merely another cruel mirage, a temptress luring us into her barren embrace?

I tightened my grip on the rusted machete, its weight a comforting anchor in this sea of desolation. Scanning the horizon with heightened senses, I cautiously took the lead, guiding our ragged band of survivors towards the crumbling ruins jutting from the sand like broken teeth. The once-great city, now a decaying remnant of a lost world, beckoned us with whispered promises of shelter and secrets.

"Stay sharp," I called back, my voice a hoarse rasp. "The dead may be absent, but danger lurks in the shadows of the forgotten."

The others murmured assent, their gazes haunted by the same specters that clawed at the edges of my mind. We had each left pieces of ourselves scattered along the blood-soaked path that led us here. Sins and sacrifices, forever etched into the hollows of our souls.

With measured steps, we navigated the sun-bleached bones of the city, the eerie silence broken only by the crunch of debris beneath our worn boots. The ghosts of the past seemed to watch from the empty windows, their judgement a palpable weight upon our weary shoulders. What right did we have to seek solace in their tomb?

I shook off the clinging tendrils of doubt, focusing on the task at hand. Survival demanded action, not reflection. The ruins held secrets, and it was up to us to unearth them, even if it meant facing the skeletons lurking in our own closets. With grim determination, I pressed forward, the weight of leadership a familiar burden as we ventured deeper into the heart of the forsaken city.

*As we ventured further into the ruins, Riku's hand found mine, her slender fingers intertwining with my calloused ones. The unexpected touch sent a jolt through my weary frame, a fleeting reminder of the humanity we clung to in this desolate world. I glanced at her, a question in my eyes, but she merely offered a silent nod, her gaze filled with a quiet understanding that words could not convey.

Together, we picked our way through the overgrown vegetation that had reclaimed the once-thriving streets. Vines snaked across crumbling facades, nature's inexorable march erasing the vestiges of a civilization long dead. The air hung heavy with the musty scent of decay, a constant reminder of the fragility of life and the inevitability of time's passage.

Our footsteps echoed in the oppressive silence, each muffled thud a testament to our presence in this forgotten place. The sound seemed to reverberate through the hollow shells of buildings, as if the city itself were whispering its secrets, daring us to uncover the truth behind its fall. I felt the weight of those secrets pressing down upon me, a burden I had carried since the world fell to ruin.

Riku's grip tightened, drawing me back from the abyss of my own thoughts. I met her gaze, seeing in her eyes a flicker of the same curiosity that gnawed at my own mind. What had become of this place? What tales lay buried beneath the rubble, waiting to be unearthed? The answers called to us, a siren song that pulled us deeper into the heart of the ruins.

But even as we pressed forward, the ghosts of our own pasts dogged our steps, their spectral fingers reaching out to drag us back into the mire of regret and sorrow. We had each left a trail of broken promises and shattered lives in our wake, the price of survival in a world where the lines between right and wrong had long since blurred. Could we ever truly outrun the sins that haunted us, or were we destined to join the ranks of the damned that wandered these forsaken streets?

A glint of sunlight caught my eye, reflecting off the cracked windows of a partially collapsed building. Its walls still stood, defiant against the ravages of time, offering a glimmer of hope amidst the desolation. I signaled to the others, my voice low and urgent. "There. We might find shelter, or something we can use."

We picked our way through the debris, the crunch of our footsteps echoing in the silence. The building loomed before us, a testament to the ingenuity of a world long gone. As we stepped through the gaping doorway, the musty scent of decay enveloped us, a reminder of the fragility of life in the face of unrelenting chaos.

Inside, the remnants of a forgotten civilization lay scattered before us. Faded paintings clung to the walls, their colors muted by the passage of years. Broken furniture littered the floor, the jagged edges of shattered wood and twisted metal reaching up like skeletal fingers. And everywhere, the belongings of those who had once called this place home - a tattered doll, a rusted locket, a shattered picture frame - each one a silent testament to the lives that had been lost.

As I moved deeper into the building, the weight of those lives pressed down upon me, their stories whispering in the shadows. Who had they been, these people whose world had been so cruelly ripped away? What dreams had they nurtured, what loves had they cherished, before the end had come? The questions haunted me, even as I pushed them aside, focusing instead on the task at hand.

But even as I searched for supplies, for anything that might aid us in our desperate struggle for survival, I couldn't shake the feeling that we were not alone. The ghosts of the past seemed to watch from every corner, their eyes boring into my soul, judging me for the choices I had made. How long could we go on like this, scavenging among the ruins of a world we had helped to destroy? How long before the weight of our own sins dragged us down into the abyss?

As I pressed onward, my heart heavy with the weight of my thoughts, Riku called out from across the room. "Maikoru, come look at this!" There was an urgency in her voice that pulled me from my reverie.

I made my way over to where she stood, her hand resting on a section of wall that looked no different from any other. But as I drew closer, I saw it - a faint seam, barely visible in the dim light. My pulse quickened as I reached out, my fingers searching for a latch or a handle.

And then, with a soft click, the hidden compartment swung open, revealing a treasure trove of preserved food and water. For a moment, I could only stare in disbelief, hardly daring to hope that this might be real. But as the others gathered around, their faces alight with a hope we had not felt in months, I knew that this was no illusion.

"We're going to make it," Riku whispered, her voice thick with emotion. "We're going to survive this, Maikoru. I know we will."

I nodded, not trusting myself to speak. But even as I reveled in this newfound hope, I couldn't shake the feeling that our struggles were far from over. For in this world of the living dead, nothing was ever certain.

We gathered what we could, filling our packs until they strained at the seams. And then, as if drawn by some unseen force, we found ourselves moving towards a crumbling staircase that led up into the unknown.

Each step felt like a leap of faith, the ancient stone crumbling beneath our feet. But still we climbed, driven by a desperate need to see what lay beyond. And as we emerged onto the upper level, the sight that greeted us took my breath away.

Through the shattered windows, the ruins of the city stretched out before us, a vast and desolate wasteland bathed in the eerie light of the setting sun. In the distance, the silhouette of a tower loomed like a sentinel, its broken spire reaching towards the heavens. And for a moment, I allowed myself to imagine what it might have been like to stand in this spot before the world had ended, to look out over a thriving metropolis full of life and promise.

But those days were gone, lost to the relentless march of time and the folly of man. Now, all that remained were the ghosts of the past and the ever-present threat of the undead. And as I gazed out over this bleak and broken landscape, I couldn't help but wonder if we were any different, just remnants of a world that had long since passed away.

My heart pounded with a sickening mix of anticipation and dread as I scanned the ruins, my eyes straining to pierce the lengthening shadows. In the fading light, every movement seemed to hold the promise of danger, every sound a harbinger of the horrors that lurked just out of sight.

"Do you see anything?" Riku whispered, her voice barely audible above the whisper of the wind.

I shook my head, my grip tightening on the weathered stock of my rifle. "Nothing yet. But that doesn't mean they're not out there, waiting for us to let our guard down."

We stood there in silence, the weight of our shared history hanging between us like a physical thing. How many times had we found ourselves in situations like this, perched on the precipice of the unknown, our lives hanging in the balance? And how many more times would we have to face the darkness before it finally consumed us?

As the sun dipped below the horizon, the shadows seemed to come alive, writhing and twisting like living things. And in that moment, I couldn't shake the feeling that we were being watched, that something ancient and malevolent had fixed its gaze upon us, biding its time until the moment was right to strike.

"We should keep moving," I said, my voice sounding hollow and distant to my own ears. "Find somewhere defensible to hole up for the night."

Riku nodded, her eyes glinting with a hardness that I had come to know all too well. Together, we turned away from the view and began to pick our way back down the crumbling staircase, the echoes of our footsteps mingling with the whispers of the dead.

But even as we descended back into the darkness, I couldn't shake the feeling that something had changed, that some fundamental shift had occurred in the very fabric of our reality. And as we made our way deeper into the ruins, I couldn't help but wonder what fresh horrors the night would bring.

The distant structure loomed larger as we approached, its crumbling walls and shattered windows a testament to the ravages of time and the relentless march of the undead. With each step, the sense of unease that had been gnawing at the back of my mind grew stronger, a palpable thing that seemed to hang in the air like a miasma.

Beside me, Riku's grip on my hand tightened, her eyes darting back and forth as she scanned the surrounding ruins for any sign of danger. I could feel the tension in her body, the coiled energy of a predator ready to strike at a moment's notice.

"Do you think it's safe?" she asked, her voice barely more than a whisper.

I shook my head, my own doubts and fears bubbling up from the depths of my soul. "I don't know," I admitted. "But we don't have a choice. We need shelter, supplies. This might be our only chance."

We reached the base of the structure, its towering walls casting long shadows across the sun-baked earth. Up close, the damage was even more apparent, the once-mighty edifice reduced to little more than a shell of its former self.

As we stepped through the gaping entrance, the air seemed to grow colder, the silence more oppressive. The hair on the back of my neck stood on end, and I could feel the weight of unseen eyes upon us, watching, waiting.

"Maikoru..." Riku's voice trembled, her fingers digging into my arm. "I have a bad feeling about this. It's like we're walking into the jaws of some great beast."

I nodded, my own heart hammering in my chest. But what choice did we have? To turn back now would be to condemn ourselves to a slow, lingering death, to the mercy of the sun and the undead.

"We'll be careful," I said, trying to inject a note of confidence into my voice. "We'll search the place quickly, grab whatever we can, and get out. Just stay close, and be ready for anything."

As we ventured deeper into the structure, the shadows seemed to come alive, reaching out with grasping fingers to pull us down into the depths of madness. And with each step, the sense of dread that had been building in my gut crescendoed to a fever pitch, until I was sure that we had crossed some invisible threshold, that we had entered a realm where the laws of nature no longer applied.

But still, we pressed on, driven by the primal need to survive, to cling to the fading light of hope in a world gone mad. And as we delved deeper into the heart of the ruins, I couldn't shake the feeling that we were being led, that some unseen force was guiding our steps towards a fate worse than death itself.

The path ahead was treacherous, the ancient stones cracked and crumbling beneath our feet. Riku's hand tightened around mine as we navigated the uneven terrain, our breaths coming in short, ragged gasps. And then we saw it, a gaping chasm where a bridge had once stood, its shattered remains scattered like broken teeth at the bottom of the ravine.

"We'll have to find another way around," I said, my voice barely above a whisper. "There's got to be..."

But my words trailed off as my gaze fell upon a narrow ledge, barely wide enough for a single person to traverse. It hugged the side of the ravine, disappearing into the shadows beyond.

"Maikoru, no," Riku pleaded, her eyes wide with fear. "It's too dangerous. We don't know what's on the other side."

I turned to face her, my hand cupping her cheek. "We don't have a choice," I said softly. "We can't go back, and we can't stay here. This is our only chance."

She searched my face for a long moment, her eyes glistening with unshed tears. And then, with a shaky nod, she let go of my hand and stepped back, allowing me to take the lead.

The ledge was even narrower than it had appeared from a distance, and the drop to the bottom of the ravine was dizzying. I pressed my back against the wall, edging forward with painstaking care, my heart pounding in my ears. Behind me, I could hear Riku's rapid breathing, the scuff of her feet against the stone.

And then, just as I was beginning to think we might make it across, I heard a sound that made my blood run cold. A low, guttural moan, echoing up from the depths of the ravine. I froze, my breath catching in my throat, as a figure emerged from the shadows below. Its flesh was rotting, its eyes milky white, its jaw hanging slack. A zombie, drawn by the sound of our passage.

I reached for my weapon, my fingers trembling as I aimed at the creature's head. But before I could pull the trigger, Riku let out a cry of warning. "Maikoru, look out!"

I whirled around, just in time to see another zombie crawling over the edge of the ravine, its fingers scrabbling for purchase on the narrow ledge. I stumbled back, my foot slipping on the edge of the precipice, and for a heart-stopping moment, I thought I was going to fall. But then Riku's hand closed around my arm, yanking me back from the brink.

We ran then, heedless of the danger, our feet pounding against the stone as we fled the horrors behind us. And as we plunged deeper into the ruins, I couldn't shake the feeling that we were being herded, that some malevolent force was guiding our steps towards an even greater horror that lay ahead.

The entrance to the underground chamber was hidden behind a curtain of vines, their leaves rustling in the faint breeze. I pulled them aside, my heart pounding as I peered into the darkness beyond. The air was thick with the stench of decay, and I could feel the weight of centuries pressing down upon me, the ghosts of the past whispering in my ear.

"Maikoru, I don't like this," Riku whispered, her hand tightening around mine. "We shouldn't go in there. We don't know what's waiting for us."

But I shook my head, steeling myself for whatever lay ahead. "We have to," I said, my voice low and urgent. "We need those supplies, Riku. Without them, we don't stand a chance."

She hesitated for a long moment, her eyes searching mine. And then, with a shaky nod, she let go of my hand and stepped back, allowing me to lead the way into the unknown.

The chamber was dark and cold, the air heavy with the weight of centuries. Our footsteps echoed off the stone walls, and I could feel the hairs on the back of my neck standing on end, as if we were being watched by unseen eyes. And then, as we rounded a corner, I saw it. A faint glimmer of light, reflecting off the surface of something metallic.

I approached cautiously, my heart pounding in my chest, my hand tightening around the hilt of my knife. And as I drew closer, I saw what it was. A cache of weapons, lying scattered across the floor. Swords, knives, bows and arrows, gleaming in the faint light. And beside them, stacked neatly in a pile, were cans of food, bottles of water, medical supplies.

For a moment, I couldn't believe what I was seeing. It was as if the gods themselves had answered our prayers, had granted us this one small mercy in a world gone mad. But even as I reached out to touch the supplies, I felt a sense of unease wash over me, a creeping dread that I couldn't quite shake.

"Maikoru," Riku whispered, her voice trembling. "Something's not right. We shouldn't be here. We need to leave, now."

But I shook my head, my mind already racing with the possibilities. With these weapons, with these supplies, we could survive. We could fight back against the undead, could carve out a new life for ourselves in this ruined world. And so, with a trembling hand, I reached out and picked up a sword, its blade gleaming in the darkness.

And as I turned to face Riku, I saw the fear in her eyes, the unspoken plea for me to reconsider. But I had made my choice, had crossed the threshold into a world where the old rules no longer applied. And as we gathered up the supplies, as we prepared to face whatever horrors lay ahead, I couldn't shake the feeling that we had just sealed our fate, that we had taken the first step down a path from which there could be no turning back.

I took a deep breath, the musty air of the chamber filling my lungs as I surveyed our newfound arsenal. Guns, ammunition, knives, and even a few grenades - a veritable treasure trove in this world where survival was the only currency that mattered. But even as I reveled in our good fortune, I couldn't shake the feeling that we were disturbing something ancient, something that should have been left untouched.

"We should take only what we need," Riku said, her voice barely above a whisper. "Leave the rest for others who may come after us."

I nodded, but my hands still lingered on the weapons, the cold metal sending a shiver down my spine. In the end, we took only what we could carry, leaving the rest behind like an offering to the ghosts of the past.

As we emerged from the chamber, blinking in the harsh sunlight, I felt a renewed sense of purpose coursing through my veins. With these weapons, we could defend ourselves against the hordes of the undead, could carve out a new life in this shattered world. But even as I clung to that hope, I couldn't shake the feeling that we had disturbed something ancient, something that should have been left alone.

"We should keep moving," I said, my voice sounding hollow in the stillness of the ruins. "Find shelter before nightfall."

Riku nodded, her hand slipping into mine as we set off once more, our footsteps echoing through the empty streets. But even as we walked, I couldn't shake the feeling that we were being watched, that the ghosts of the past were following us, waiting for the right moment to strike.

And so we walked, the weight of our sins heavy on our shoulders, the memory of the chamber and its secrets haunting our every step. For in this world, there was no escape from the horrors of the past, no redemption for the choices we had made. We could only keep moving forward, one step at a time, until the end finally came for us all.

The sun scorched our backs as Riku and I surveyed the tribe's progress, their ragged forms shuffling among the ruins. Skeletal fingers of steel jutted from crumbling concrete, a graveyard of a once-great city now repurposed for our meager shelters.

"You there," I barked at a hunched figure. "Gather more rebar from the collapsed overpass. And you, salvage those sheets of corrugated metal." They nodded wearily, eyes haunted by horrors I could only imagine.

As I turned, a flash of movement caught my eye. Children, their faces smudged with grime, darted between shadowed doorways, giggling. A cold dread crept up my spine. "Riku," I hissed. "Watch the others. I need to...take care of something."

I approached the little ones, their playful chatter echoing in the hollow city. Memories stabbed at me, ghosts of the innocents I failed to protect. "You can't be here," I said, fighting to keep my voice steady. "It's not safe."

"But we found something shiny!" a little girl chirped, eyes wide.

My blood ran cold. Relics of the old world often promised only suffering. "Show me," I commanded.

They led me into the crumbling husk of a toy store, dusty trinkets strewn across buckled floors. The girl held up a dented music box, its faded ballerina still pirouetting. A lump formed in my throat.

"It's lovely," I lied. "But we have to go. Now." I herded them out, casting wary glances at every shadow. This city had taken everything from me once. I wouldn't let it take the children too.

As we emerged into the blistering heat, I saw Riku approaching, his brow creased with worry. "Everything alright?"

I nodded curtly. "It will be. As long as we remember...nowhere is safe. Not anymore."

The ghosts pressed close, whispering their accusations. I shoved them away, back into the dark recesses of my mind. There would be time enough to face my sins. But not today. Today, we had shelters to build and a tribe to protect. The dead would have to wait.

The sun beat down mercilessly as Riku and I led a small team into the desert valley, our throats parched and our spirits flagging. We had to find water, and soon, or all our efforts to rebuild would be for naught.

I scanned the barren landscape, searching for any sign of life amidst the endless sea of sand. The ghosts of the old world mocked me, their laughter echoing in the hollow spaces of my mind. "You're chasing mirages," they taunted. "There's nothing out here but death."

I gritted my teeth and pressed on, refusing to let their whispers sway me. We had come too far to give up now.

Suddenly, Riku grabbed my arm, his eyes wide with disbelief. "Look," he breathed, pointing to a distant shimmering on the horizon.

I squinted against the glare, hardly daring to hope. But there it was - a small pool of water, nestled among a cluster of lush vegetation. An oasis in the midst of the wasteland.

We approached cautiously, half-expecting it to vanish like a mirage. But the water was real, cool and clear and more precious than gold. We drank deeply, savoring every drop, and filled our canteens to bursting.

"We have to tell the others," Riku said, his voice hoarse with emotion. "This could change everything."

I nodded, my own eyes stinging with unshed tears. For the first time in months, I allowed myself to feel a flicker of hope. Perhaps we weren't doomed to wander this blighted earth forever. Perhaps there was still a chance for something more.

As we made our way back to the ruins, I couldn't shake the feeling that we were being watched. The ghosts of my past dogged my every step, their accusations growing louder with each passing moment. "You don't deserve this," they hissed. "You'll only lead them to ruin, just like before."

I pushed their voices aside, focusing instead on the task at hand. We had water now, but we still needed food. The tribe was depending on us.

We picked our way through the crumbling remains of the city, every shadow a potential threat. I kept one hand on my weapon, ready to defend against any danger that might lurk in the ruins.

And then I saw it - a hidden cache of preserved food, tucked away in the corner of a collapsed storefront. Cans of beans, packets of dried fruit, even a few precious bars of chocolate. It was a treasure trove beyond our wildest dreams.

I shared the discovery with the others, watching their faces light up with relief and gratitude. For a moment, the ghosts fell silent, drowned out by the jubilant exclamations of the tribe.

But I knew they would be back. They always were. The sins of my past were a heavy burden to bear, and I couldn't shake the feeling that I was leading these people down a path to destruction.

Still, I had to try. For Riku, for the children, for the faint hope of a future that didn't end in blood and ashes. I would keep fighting, keep pushing forward, even if it meant facing the ghosts that haunted me at every turn.

Because in this bleak and broken world, hope was the only currency that mattered. And I would cling to it with every last shred of my being, no matter the cost.

As the sun dipped below the horizon, painting the sky in shades of orange and red, we gathered around the makeshift fire pit. The flames cast a flickering light over the faces of the tribe, illuminating the weariness and desperation that had become our constant companions.

I watched as they shared stories of their past lives, their voices barely above a whisper. Tales of loved ones lost, of dreams shattered, of a world that had once been filled with beauty and promise. Each word was a twist of the knife in my gut, a reminder of all that we had lost.

But as the night wore on, something began to shift. The stories turned from sorrow to resilience, from despair to determination. I listened as they spoke of the small victories we had achieved, of the way we had come together in the face of unimaginable adversity.

"We may have lost everything," I found myself saying, my voice raw with emotion. "But we still have each other. And as long as we hold onto that, as long as we keep fighting, there is still hope."

The words felt hollow even as I spoke them, but I could see the effect they had on the others. Backs straightened, eyes brightened, and for a moment, the ghosts that haunted us all seemed to recede into the shadows.

Later, as the fire died down to embers, Riku and I ventured deeper into the ruins. We picked our way through the rubble, our footsteps echoing in the eerie silence. I couldn't shake the feeling that we were being watched, that the ghosts of the past were lurking just out of sight.

And then we found it - a crumbling library, its shelves still lined with books. Most were too damaged to salvage, their pages crumbling to dust at the slightest touch. But a few had survived, their covers still intact.

I reached for one with trembling hands, my heart pounding in my chest. The weight of it was a comfort, a tangible reminder of the knowledge and history that had once been so easily taken for granted.

"We'll take them back to the tribe," I said, my voice barely above a whisper. "Preserve what we can, pass it down to the next generation."

Riku nodded, her eyes glinting with a fierce determination. "We'll rebuild," she said. "No matter how long it takes, no matter what we have to face. We'll find a way."

I wanted to believe her, wanted to cling to that fragile hope with every fiber of my being. But even as we made our way back to the others, the books clutched tightly to our chests, I couldn't shake the feeling that the ghosts were still watching, waiting for their moment to strike.

The winds came without warning, a howling fury that tore through our makeshift shelters like they were made of paper. I staggered against the onslaught, my eyes stinging with sand as I tried to rally the others.

"Get to the sturdy structures!" I shouted above the roar of the storm. "Hurry!"

Riku was at my side in an instant, her hand gripping mine with a fierce intensity. Together, we herded the tribe towards the buildings we had reinforced, praying they would hold against the relentless assault of the sandstorm.

We huddled together in the darkness, listening to the wind scream and howl like a living thing. I could feel the weight of their fear, the trembling of their bodies pressed close to mine. *What if this is the end?* the insidious voice in my mind whispered. *What if all our efforts have been for nothing?*

But I couldn't let myself give in to despair. I had to be strong, for Riku, for the tribe. We had come too far to let a storm defeat us now.

It felt like an eternity before the winds finally died down, before we dared to emerge from our shelter. The sight that greeted us was one of devastation - our crops, so carefully tended, lay flattened and broken, the earth scoured clean by the relentless sands.

"No," Riku whispered, her voice breaking. "All our hard work..."

I drew her close, feeling the shudder of her breath against my chest. "We'll find a way," I murmured, echoing her earlier words. "We always do."

Together, we surveyed the damage, our minds racing as we tried to formulate a plan. The crops were a vital source of sustenance, and without them, we would be forced to rely even more heavily on our dwindling supplies.

"Barriers," I said at last, my voice rough with exhaustion. "We'll build barriers around the remaining crops, try to protect them from future storms."

Riku nodded, her jaw set with determination. "And irrigation," she added. "We'll dig channels, redirect water from the oasis to keep the soil moist."

It wouldn't be easy, but nothing in this harsh new world ever was. We had to adapt, to innovate, to find ways to survive against all odds.

As we set to work, the sun beating down mercilessly overhead, I couldn't shake the feeling that the storm had been a warning, a reminder of the fragility of our existence. We were all walking a razor's edge, balanced precariously between life and death.

But we're still here, I reminded myself, my hands blistering as I dug trenches in the unyielding earth. *We're still fighting.* And as long as we had each other, as long as we held on to hope, I knew we would never stop.

The sun hung low on the horizon, casting long shadows across the barren landscape as we set out on our hunt. Riku and I led the way, our steps sure and silent, the rest of the hunting party fanning out behind us. We had to be cautious, alert for any signs of danger, whether from the undead or the unpredictable wildlife that roamed these parts.

We need this, I thought grimly, my fingers tightening around the worn grip of my spear. *The tribe needs this.* With our crops damaged and our supplies running low, a successful hunt could mean the difference between survival and starvation.

The heat was oppressive, the air shimmering with mirages that danced tantalizingly on the edge of our vision. But we pressed on, driven by a primal instinct to provide for our people.

It was Riku who spotted the tracks first, her keen eyes picking out the faint impressions in the sand. "Boar," she said softly, crouching down to examine the marks more closely. "A small group, from the looks of it."

I nodded, a flicker of hope kindling in my chest. If we could bring down even one of the beasts, it would go a long way toward feeding the tribe.

We followed the tracks, moving with a silent intensity, our senses heightened by the thrill of the hunt. And then, as we crested a small rise, we saw them: a cluster of wild boars, rooting in the sparse vegetation at the base of a cliff.

"Spread out," I whispered to the others, motioning for them to circle around to the other side of the creatures. "We'll drive them towards the cliff face, cut off their escape."

It was a risky plan, but one born of desperation. We had to make this count.

With a swift, coordinated attack, we charged the boars, our spears flashing in the fading light. The beasts squealed in terror, scattering in all directions, but we had them trapped. One by one, we brought them down, until at last, a single massive boar lay at our feet, its lifeblood staining the sand.

"Well done," I said, my voice ragged with exhaustion and relief. "This will feed the tribe for days."

But even as we celebrated our victory, I couldn't shake the sense of unease that crept along my spine. The hunt had been too easy, the boars too slow and clumsy. It was as if they, too, were weakened by the harsh realities of this new world.

What else is out there, I wondered, *waiting in the shadows, ready to strike when we least expect it?*

As we made our way back to the camp, the carcass of the boar slung between us, the weight of responsibility settled heavily on my shoulders. We had survived another day, but the future remained uncertain, a yawning void of possibilities both terrifying and exhilarating.

The mood back at the camp was subdued, the joy of our successful hunt tempered by the ongoing struggles we faced. Tensions were running high, the stress of the constant battle for survival wearing on even the strongest among us.

I watched as two of the younger men argued heatedly over the distribution of the boar meat, their voices rising in anger and frustration. It was a scene that had become all too familiar in recent days, as the strain of our situation began to take its toll.

We can't go on like this, I thought wearily, stepping forward to intervene before the argument could escalate further. *We have to find a way to come together, to work as one, or we'll tear ourselves apart from the inside out.*

"Enough," I said firmly, positioning myself between the two men. "We're all in this together, and we all have a right to share in the spoils of the hunt. There's no place for greed or selfishness here, not if we want to survive."

The men glared at each other for a moment longer, and then reluctantly stepped back, their anger still simmering beneath the surface.

I turned to address the rest of the tribe, my voice ringing out across the camp. "We've faced challenges before, and we'll face them again. But we can't let them divide us. We have to remember what's important: our unity, our strength as a community. That's what will see us through, no matter what comes our way."

It's a pretty speech, a small, cynical voice whispered in the back of my mind. *But will it be enough? Can words alone hold back the tide of fear and desperation that threatens to engulf us all?*

But I pushed those thoughts aside, focusing instead on the faces of my people, on the flickers of hope and determination that still shone in their eyes. We had come too far, endured too much, to give up now.

Communicate, I reminded myself. *Keep them talking, keep them connected. It's the only way we'll survive.*

I followed the twisting, rubble-strewn passageway, my heart pounding in my chest. The air grew colder as we descended, and I could feel the weight of centuries pressing down upon us. Riku's footsteps echoed behind me, a steady rhythm in the darkness.

And then, suddenly, the passage opened up into a vast chamber. I lifted my torch, its flickering light revealing rows of ancient artifacts, their surfaces gleaming dully in the shadows. Crumbling statues stood sentinel along the walls, their faces worn smooth by the passage of time.

"What is this place?" Riku breathed, her voice hushed with awe.

I shook my head, unable to find words. It was like stepping into another world, a forgotten realm untouched by the ravages of the apocalypse. I moved forward slowly, my fingers trailing over the artifacts. Each one seemed to hold a story, a fragment of the past waiting to be unleashed.

What secrets do they hold? I wondered. *What tales of the world that was, before everything fell apart?*

But before I could ponder further, a shrill scream pierced the air. I whirled around, my heart in my throat. The scream came again, echoing through the ruins above.

"The tribe," Riku gasped. "They're under attack."

We raced up the passageway, our feet pounding against the stone. I emerged into chaos, the air thick with the stench of rotting flesh. Zombies swarmed through the camp, their growls mingling with the screams of the survivors.

I leapt into the fray, my machete flashing in the sunlight. Riku was at my side, her sword singing as it cleaved through the horde. We fought with a ferocity born of desperation, our movements a deadly dance.

Protect them, a voice whispered in my mind. *They're all that's left, all that matters.*

I lost myself in the battle, my world narrowing to the slash of my blade and the snarls of the undead. Time seemed to stretch and twist, seconds bleeding into hours. But still, we fought on, driven by the knowledge that if we fell, the tribe would fall with us.

How many more? I thought numbly, my arms aching with fatigue. *How many more must we kill before it's over?*

But there was no end in sight, no respite from the relentless tide of death. And so we fought, two lone warriors against an army of the damned, hoping against hope that somehow, we would prevail.

At last, the final zombie fell, its skull smashed by the butt of my machete. I stood there, chest heaving, blood dripping from my blade. Riku sagged against me, her sword clattering to the ground.

"Maikoru," she whispered, her voice hoarse. "Are you...?"

I pulled her into my arms, burying my face in her hair. "I'm here," I murmured. "I'm with you."

We clung to each other amidst the carnage, drawing strength from the warmth of our embrace. In that moment, nothing else mattered - not the ruins that surrounded us, not the horrors we had faced. Only the beating of our hearts, the knowledge that we had survived.

But for how long? a traitorous voice whispered in my mind. *How long until the next attack, the next battle?*

I pushed the thought away, focusing instead on the woman in my arms. Riku was my anchor, my reason for fighting. Without her, I would be lost, adrift in a sea of despair.

Slowly, reluctantly, we pulled apart. I turned to face the tribe, their faces a mix of fear and relief. They looked to me for guidance, for reassurance.

I took a deep breath, my voice ringing out across the ruins. "We have faced much, my friends," I said. "We have lost much. But we are still here, still fighting. And as long as we stand together, as long as we hold on to hope, we will prevail."

I saw the flicker of determination in their eyes, the spark of resilience that refused to be extinguished. They nodded, their backs straightening, their hands tightening on their weapons.

"We will rebuild," I continued, my voice growing stronger. "We will create a new life, a new future, amidst these ruins. And we will never, never give up."

A cheer went up from the tribe, their voices echoing off the crumbling walls. I felt a surge of pride, of love for these people who had become my family.

We will survive, I vowed silently. *No matter what horrors this world throws at us, we will endure.*

And with that thought, I turned to face the ruins once more, ready to begin anew.

The city lay in ruins before me, a graveyard of shattered glass and crumbling concrete. I perched atop a fallen skyscraper, surveying the desolation—my kingdom of dust and decay. Home. What a strange concept now, in this bleak hellscape the world had become.

Unbidden, memories crept into my troubled mind like tangled vines, choked with grief. Images of the lush, verdant rainforest flickered behind my eyes. Our peaceful village, nestled beneath the green canopy. A sanctuary.

All gone now. Consumed. Just like everything else.

I gulped a ragged breath, swallowing the bitter nostalgia that coated my tongue. The sun glared mercilessly down, bleaching the color from this wretched desert valley we now called home. A mockery. A cruel joke.

"Home," I muttered, the word tasting like ash in my parched mouth. "This is home now. This blasted wasteland."

My tribe looked to me to guide them, to keep them safe. But how could I protect anyone in this godforsaken ruin? When death and horror lurked around every jagged corner? When the relentless sun scorched all hope from our hearts?

I clenched my fists until my knuckles blanched bone-white. No. I would not falter or fail them. No matter the cost to my own damned soul. This was our home now. And I would make it one, even if it killed me.

Even if we had to build a new life atop the corpses of the undead.

The bonds we'd forged in blood and tears, in desperate battles against the ravenous hordes - those were the threads that held us together now. The only thing that kept us from unraveling completely.

I thought of Riku, my rock, my solace in this unending nightmare. Her gentle touch, her unwavering faith in me, even when I had none in myself. She was the light that kept the shadows at bay, the soothing balm to my tortured mind.

And the others - Kira, with her fierce determination. Hiro, with his unwavering loyalty. Nao, with her sharp wit that could cut through the darkest despair. They were more than just survivors, more than just a tribe.

They were family.

In the midst of the apocalypse, we had found something precious, something worth fighting for. Worth dying for. The laughter we shared over meager meals, the tears we shed for fallen comrades, the triumphs we celebrated as one - those moments, fleeting as they were, had become our lifeblood.

The world might have ended, but our bonds endured. Unbreakable. Forged in the crucible of this hellish existence.

I closed my eyes, letting the weight of those connections settle over me like a tattered cloak. It was a heavy burden, but one I would bear gladly. For them. For our family.

For our home.

The desert winds howled, a mournful dirge that echoed the ache in my bones. But beneath the sorrow, beneath the pain, a flicker of something else took root.

Hope.

Fragile, tenuous, but there nonetheless. A stubborn weed pushing through the cracks of a shattered world.

We would survive this. We would build a new life, a new home, from the ashes of the old. Together.

Always together.

But even as that flicker of hope burned within me, the shadows of doubt crept in, insidious and relentless. The weight of leadership pressed down upon my shoulders, a burden that threatened to crush me beneath its unforgiving mass.

Was I truly capable of guiding them through this nightmare? Could I keep them safe, keep them alive, in a world where death lurked around every corner?

I had failed before. Failed to save those who looked to me for protection. Their faces haunted me still, accusing specters that lingered in the dark recesses of my mind.

How could I be the leader they needed, when I was so utterly broken?

My hands trembled, and I clenched them into fists, willing the weakness away. But it persisted, a festering wound that refused to heal.

"Maikoru?" Riku's voice, soft and concerned, cut through the haze of self-doubt. "Are you alright?"

I forced a smile, but it felt brittle, like it might shatter at any moment. "I'm fine, Riku. Just... thinking."

She studied me, her gaze piercing, as if she could see straight through my flimsy façade. "You don't have to carry this burden alone, you know. We're all in this together."

Together. The word echoed in my mind, a lifeline in the darkness.

I thought of the sacrifices they had made, the resilience they had shown in the face of unimaginable horror. Kira, fighting through her grief to become a fierce warrior. Hiro, risking his life to protect the weak and the vulnerable. Nao, finding humor in the bleakest of moments, a light in the darkness.

They were the reason I kept going, the reason I couldn't give up.

I drew in a deep breath, letting their strength flow through me, bolstering my own. "You're right, Riku. We are in this together. And together, we'll find a way through this. We have to."

For a moment, the doubts receded, pushed back by the force of my resolve. I would not let them down. I could not let them down.

We would survive. We would build a new home, a new future, from the ashes of the old.

And I would lead them there, even if it cost me everything.

The specter of our past lives haunted me, the memories of what we'd lost, what we'd sacrificed, clawing at the edges of my mind. But I couldn't let them drag me under, not now, not when they needed me most.

I stood, my legs unsteady beneath me, and turned to face the ruins that stretched out before us. The sun-scorched earth, the crumbling buildings, the eerie silence that hung heavy in the air. This was our world now, our reality.

But it wouldn't be forever.

I closed my eyes, letting the vision take shape in my mind. A future where we thrived, where we adapted to this new world, where we built something lasting from the rubble of the old. It seemed like an impossible dream, a foolish hope, but I clung to it like a lifeline.

"We'll make this place our own," I said, my voice steady despite the tremor in my hands. "We'll learn to live in this new world, to make it work for us. We'll create a home, a community, a place where we can be safe, where we can build something that lasts."

Riku stepped up beside me, her presence a comfort, a reminder that I wasn't alone. "It won't be easy," she said quietly. "But we've come this far. We can't give up now."

I nodded, my jaw tight with determination. "We won't give up. We'll fight for this future, for our people, for the home we deserve. And we'll win, no matter what it takes."

The words tasted like ashes on my tongue, but I forced them out anyway. They needed to hear them, needed to believe in the possibility of a better tomorrow, even if I couldn't quite believe it myself.

I turned to face them, my gaze sweeping over the ragged group of survivors who had become my family, my reason for living. They looked back at me, their eyes filled with a mix of hope and fear, trust and uncertainty.

"We are the last of humanity," I said, my voice ringing out across the ruins. "And we will not be defeated. We will rise from these ashes, stronger than before. We will build a new world, a better world, and we will do it together."

A cheer went up from the crowd, a sound of defiance, of determination, of hope. I let it wash over me, letting it bolster my resolve, my strength.

We would survive. We would thrive. And I would lead them there, no matter the cost.

As the cheers died down, I felt a gentle hand on my shoulder. I turned to see Riku, her eyes shimmering with unshed tears. "Maikoru," she whispered, her voice barely audible above the wind. "You don't have to carry this burden alone. I'm here for you, always."

I swallowed hard, my throat tight with emotion. "I know," I murmured, reaching up to cover her hand with my own. "And I'm grateful for that, more than you could ever know."

She smiled then, a rare, precious thing in this bleak world. "We're in this together," she said, her fingers intertwining with mine. "Through whatever lies ahead."

I nodded, drawing strength from her touch, from the love and devotion that radiated from her very being. With Riku by my side, I felt like I could face anything, even the darkest of nightmares.

I turned back to the horizon, my gaze fixed on the setting sun. The sky was a blaze of orange and red, as if the world itself was on fire. But beneath the chaos, beneath the destruction, there was a glimmer of something else, something that I had almost forgotten existed.

Hope.

It was a fragile thing, a flickering flame in the darkness. But it was there, burning bright within the hearts of my people, within the heart of the woman who stood beside me.

And as I watched the sun sink below the horizon, I knew that we would keep that flame alive, no matter what the future held. We would fight for it, bleed for it, die for it if we had to.

Because in the end, hope was all we had left.

And I would be damned if I let it slip away.

My gaze lingered on the banner, a tattered remnant of the world we once knew. The fabric fluttered in the evening breeze, its colors faded and worn, yet still defiant against the relentless march of decay. It was a symbol of our resilience, our refusal to submit to the undead scourge that had consumed everything we held dear.

I took a deep breath, the air thick with the stench of rot and despair. The sun was setting, casting an eerie glow over the desolate landscape, the shadows lengthening like grasping fingers. It was a reminder of the darkness that always lurked just beyond the light, waiting to swallow us whole.

But I refused to let it consume me, to let it consume us. We had come too far, fought too hard, to surrender now. I had a duty to my people, to the survivors who looked to me for guidance and protection. I could not falter, could not let my own doubts and fears overshadow the needs of the many.

"Maikoru?" Riku's voice, soft and concerned, pulled me from my thoughts. "Are you alright?"

I turned to face her, my lips curving into a weary smile. "I'm fine," I lied, the words tasting bitter on my tongue. "Just thinking about what comes next."

She studied me for a moment, her eyes searching mine for the truth I tried to hide. "You don't have to carry this burden alone," she said, her hand coming to rest on my shoulder. "We're all here for you, you know that, right?"

I nodded, the weight of her touch grounding me in the present. "I know," I said, my voice barely above a whisper. "But I'm the leader. It's my responsibility to keep us safe, to find a way forward."

"And you will," she said, her faith in me unwavering. "But you don't have to do it alone. We're stronger together, Maikoru. Always have been, always will be."

I looked out over the ruins of the city, the once-towering skyscrapers now crumbling monuments to a forgotten age. The sun had almost disappeared below the horizon, the last rays of light painting the sky in shades of blood and fire.

It was a fitting metaphor for the world we lived in now, a world where the line between life and death had blurred beyond recognition. But even in the midst of such darkness, there was still a flicker of hope, a spark of something better waiting to be kindled.

And as I stood there, Riku by my side, the banner of our tribe fluttering above us, I knew that it was my duty to nurture that spark, to fan it into a flame that could light the way forward.

For my people. For our future.

For the home we would build together, even in the midst of the apocalypse.

I awoke with a start, my heart pounding as the nightmares of the undead clawing at our walls slowly faded into the grim reality of another day in this hellscape. The first pale fingers of dawn crept through the gaps between the rotting boards, casting a ghostly light over Riku's sleeping form beside me. As if sensing my gaze, her eyelids fluttered open, and for a fleeting moment, the love and tenderness in her eyes chased away the ever-present dread that haunted me. How long could we keep pretending there was still hope, still a future, in this blighted world?

With a heavy sigh, I dragged myself upright, my body aching with the weight of too many battles, too many losses. The floorboards creaked mournfully beneath my feet as I shuffled over to the makeshift workbench in the corner. Methodically, almost meditatively, I began the now-familiar routine - examining my blades for nicks and dullness, honing the edges against the whetstone until they gleamed with lethal sharpness.

Behind me, I could hear Riku murmuring softly to Hana and Takeshi as she roused them for the day ahead. "Come now darlings, up you get. Let's see what treats Papa brought us back last night, shall we?"

I smiled wryly to myself, marveling at her ability to muster cheer and optimism, even now. She was always the strong one, my rock and my light in the darkness. I didn't deserve her. How much blood stained my hands, how many sins shackled my soul? And yet she stayed by my side, believing in me, pulling me back from the brink of despair time and again.

Satisfied my weapons would serve me well for another day, I turned my attention to the traps I had laid out the night before, hoping against hope that some hapless creature had stumbled into them, granting us a precious reprieve from the gnawing hunger that was our constant companion these days. Each one I checked was as I had left it, taunting me with its barrenness. I could feel the frustration rising like bile in my throat, the helplessness, the fury at the cruel gods that had forsaken us to this miserable existence.

But I couldn't let them see me falter, couldn't let the cracks in my facade show. For Riku, for the little ones, I had to be strong, had to keep going, even when all I wanted was to lay down my burdens and rest. Schooling my features into some approximation of a hopeful smile, I returned to my family, steeling myself for another day in our purgatory.

"No luck with the snares, I'm afraid. But don't worry, I'll find us something. I always do, don't I?"

Riku's eyes met mine across the flickering flames of our small fire, a knowing look passing between us. She could see through my forced optimism, could sense the desperation that lurked just beneath the surface. But she wouldn't call me on it, not now, not in front of the children. Instead, she nodded, her lips curving into a smile that didn't quite reach her eyes.

"Of course you will, my love. We have faith in you."

The words were meant to be reassuring, but they felt like a lead weight upon my shoulders. Their faith in me, their reliance on my ability to provide, to protect... it was a burden I feared I could no longer bear. But what choice did I have? In this world, in this life, we only had each other.

As if sensing the dark turn of my thoughts, Riku reached out, her hand finding mine across the fire. Her touch was warm, grounding, a lifeline in the tempest of my mind. "We'll make it through this, Maikoru. Together. Just like we always have."

I wanted to believe her, wanted to cling to that hope like a drowning man to a raft. But the moans that carried on the wind, the shuffling of feet in the distance... they were a constant reminder of the horrors that lurked just beyond the fragile safety of our home.

"Do you ever wonder what it would be like, to live without this constant fear?" I asked, my voice barely above a whisper. "To not have to worry about where our next meal will come from, or whether we'll survive another night?"

Riku was silent for a long moment, the dancing flames casting shadows across her face. When she spoke, her words were heavy with the weight of all we had endured. "I do. But then I look at our children, at the love we share, and I know that even in this hell, we have something worth fighting for. Something worth living for."

Her words struck a chord within me, igniting a spark of determination that had nearly been extinguished by the relentless hardships of our existence. She was right. Our love, our family... they were the only things that mattered now. And I would do whatever it took to keep them safe, to give them a future beyond this nightmare.

The distant moans grew louder, the shuffling more pronounced. Riku's hand tightened around mine, her eyes hardening with resolve.

No words were needed. We both knew what we had to do, what we would always do.

Protect our own. No matter the cost.

I stepped out into the desolate landscape, the weight of responsibility heavy on my shoulders. The sun, a cruel and unforgiving presence, beat down upon the scorched earth, casting long shadows that seemed to writhe with a life of their own. I moved with cautious steps, my senses heightened, ever vigilant for the slightest sign of danger.

The ruins of the old world loomed before me, a haunting reminder of all that had been lost. Shattered windows and crumbling walls spoke of a time when life had thrived, when the streets had been filled with the sounds of laughter and the bustle of everyday existence. Now, only the eerie silence remained, broken only by the occasional moan of the undead.

I pressed onward, my heart heavy with the knowledge that Riku and our children were counting on me. Each step was a battle against the fear that gnawed at my soul, the constant whisper of doubt that questioned whether we would ever find a place to call home again.

As I approached an abandoned building, a flicker of hope stirred within me. The structure appeared untouched by the ravages of time, its walls still standing strong against the onslaught of decay. With a trembling hand, I reached for the door, my breath caught in my throat as I stepped inside.

And there, in the dimly lit interior, I saw it. A hidden cache of supplies, a treasure trove of items that could sustain us for weeks, perhaps even months. Canned goods, medical supplies, and even a few precious bottles of clean water. It was a miracle, a blessing in a world where such things had become rarer than gold.

I carefully gathered the supplies, my hands shaking with a mixture of relief and disbelief. As I loaded them into my backpack, I couldn't help but wonder at the twist of fate that had led me to this discovery.

Was it mere chance, or was there some greater force at work, guiding me to this moment?

"Thank you," I whispered, my words echoing in the emptiness of the building. "Thank you for this gift, for this chance to keep my family alive."

But even as I spoke the words, I knew that our struggles were far from over. The road ahead would be long and treacherous, filled with countless dangers and challenges. Yet in that moment, with the weight of the supplies on my back and the knowledge that I had provided for my loved ones, I felt a flicker of something I had almost forgotten.

Hope.

And with that hope, I stepped back out into the unforgiving world, ready to face whatever lay ahead. For Riku, for our children, I would keep fighting, keep searching for a way to build a life amidst the ruins of the old world.

No matter the cost.

The haunting moans of the undead shattered the fragile peace of our sanctuary, their shuffling steps drawing ever closer. I watched, my heart in my throat, as Riku's keen senses detected the approaching threat. Her eyes, once soft with love, now hardened with a fierce determination.

"Maikoru, they're coming," she said, her voice steady despite the fear that lurked beneath the surface. "We have to protect the children."

I nodded, my grip tightening on the weapon at my side. "I'll hold them off. Get the kids inside, now."

Riku hesitated for a moment, her gaze locked with mine. In that fleeting glance, a lifetime of love and sacrifice passed between us. Then, with a quick nod, she turned and ushered our children into the dwelling, her movements swift and purposeful.

As I watched them disappear inside, a cold sense of dread settled over me. The supplies I had found, the hope they had kindled, now seemed like a distant memory. In this moment, all that mattered was the survival of my family.

The moans grew louder, the stench of decaying flesh filling the air. I turned to face the horde, my weapon at the ready. They came into view, a shambling mass of rotting bodies and soulless eyes. My heart raced, my breath coming in short, ragged gasps.

"Please, let them be safe," I whispered, a desperate prayer to any god that might still listen.

I charged forward, my weapon slicing through the air. The first of the undead fell, its skull shattered by the force of my blow. But there were more, always more, an endless tide of horror and despair.

Behind me, I heard the sound of scraping and pounding as Riku barricaded the entrance to our home. The weight of my responsibility pressed down on me, a suffocating burden. I had to keep fighting, had to give her time to secure our children.

The battle raged on, my body moving with a primal grace born of desperation and love. Each strike was a testament to my resolve, each fallen corpse a step closer to my family's safety. But even as I fought, I could feel my strength waning, my hope dimming.

"Maikoru!" Riku's voice cut through the chaos, a beacon in the darkness. She emerged from the dwelling, her own weapon in hand, and joined me in the fray.

Together, we danced a macabre waltz, our movements perfectly synchronized. We had fought this battle countless times before, each scar a reminder of the sacrifices we had made. But this time felt different, the stakes higher than ever before.

As the last of the undead fell, we stood amid the carnage, our chests heaving with exertion. Riku's hand found mine, her fingers intertwining with my own. In that moment, I felt a flicker of the love that had sustained us through the darkest of times.

"We did it," she whispered, her voice barely audible above the pounding of my heart. "We kept them safe."

I nodded, too exhausted to speak. But as I looked into Riku's eyes, I saw the same fear that haunted my own soul. We had won this battle, but the war was far from over. In this world of endless horror, there was no true safety, no lasting peace.

And so, with heavy hearts and trembling hands, we turned back to our dwelling, ready to face whatever nightmares the future held. For in this land of the dead, love was the only thing that kept us alive.

As we stepped back into our dwelling, the weight of our reality settled upon our shoulders once more. The children huddled together, their eyes wide with fear and uncertainty. Riku gathered them close, whispering words of comfort that rang hollow even to my ears.

I turned away, unable to bear the sight of their innocence slowly being chipped away by the horrors of this world. Instead, I focused on the task at hand, reinforcing the barricades and checking our dwindling supplies.

The silence was suffocating, broken only by the distant moans of the undead and the soft whimpers of our children. I longed for the days when laughter filled our home, when the future held promise instead of despair.

As night fell, we gathered around the flickering light of a single candle, its warmth a pitiful defense against the darkness that pressed in from all sides. Riku's voice, once so full of life, now sounded weary and strained as she told stories of our ancestors, of a time when the world was not a living nightmare.

I watched the shadows dance across the walls, my mind haunted by the memories of those we had lost. How many more would we have to bury before this nightmare ended? How long could we cling to the tattered remnants of our humanity?

As the candle sputtered and died, we lay in the darkness, our bodies intertwined, seeking comfort in each other's presence. But even as I held Riku close, I could feel the weight of our burdens slowly crushing us both.

Sleep eluded me, my mind plagued by the knowledge that each day brought us closer to the inevitable. In this world, there were no happy endings, no fairy tale rescues. There was only survival, and the desperate hope that somehow, against all odds, we would find a way to keep our family alive.

But as the first rays of dawn crept through the cracks in our walls, I knew that hope was a luxury we could no longer afford. The only thing left to us was the grim determination to face another day, to fight and bleed and suffer for the chance to see another sunrise.

And so, with a heavy heart and a soul stained by the blood of the innocent, I rose to meet the challenges that lay ahead, knowing that in this world of endless horror, there was no other choice.

As the first light of dawn crept through the cracks in our walls, I rose from our makeshift bed, my body aching from the battle the day before. Riku stirred beside me, her eyes fluttering open, the weight of our reality settling upon her once more.

"We need to fortify the barricades," I said, my voice rough with exhaustion. "We can't afford another close call like yesterday."

Riku nodded, her gaze hardening with determination. "I'll check the traps and see if we caught anything overnight. The children will be hungry."

We set to work, our movements precise and efficient, honed by months of practice. I hauled broken furniture and debris to reinforce the walls, while Riku mended torn clothing and sharpened our blades.

As I worked, my thoughts drifted to the stories my father used to tell me, tales of our ancestors who had faced their own trials and emerged victorious. But in this world, where the dead walked and the living were little more than prey, those stories felt like a cruel mockery.

"Do you think they ever felt like this?" I asked, my voice barely above a whisper. "Our ancestors, I mean. Do you think they ever wondered if they were fighting a losing battle?"

Riku paused, her eyes meeting mine across the room. "I think they did what they had to do to survive, just like we're doing now. They fought because they had no other choice, because giving up meant death."

I nodded, the weight of her words settling heavy on my shoulders. We were the inheritors of a legacy of survival, a lineage of warriors who had refused to succumb to despair.

As night fell, we gathered our children close, huddling around the faint glow of a single candle. In the flickering light, I could see the fear in their eyes, the unspoken questions that lurked behind their innocent faces.

"Let me tell you a story," I began, my voice low and steady. "A story of our people, of the warriors who came before us and the battles they fought to keep our tribe alive."

And so, as the darkness pressed in around us, I wove a tale of courage and sacrifice, of heroes who had faced impossible odds and emerged victorious. I spoke of the traditions that had sustained our people for generations, the values that had given us strength in the face of unimaginable horror.

But even as the words left my lips, I could feel the hollowness in my chest, the gnawing doubt that threatened to consume me. How many more stories would we have to tell, how many more lies would we have to spin, to keep our children from succumbing to despair? How many more graves...

As the story came to an end, I felt Riku's hand slip into mine, her fingers intertwining with my own. In the warmth of her touch, I found a glimmer of hope, a reminder of the love that had sustained us through the darkest of times.

We settled into our makeshift beds, the children curled up beside us, their small bodies seeking comfort and protection. I pulled Riku close, burying my face in the crook of her neck, breathing in the scent of her skin.

"We'll make it through this," I whispered, my lips brushing against her ear. "We'll find a way to keep our family safe, to preserve our way of life."

Riku's arms tightened around me, her voice a soft murmur in the darkness. "I know we will, my love. Together, we can face anything."

But even as we clung to each other, I could feel the weight of the past pressing down upon us, the memories of all we had lost, all we had sacrificed. The night was filled with the distant moans of the undead, a haunting chorus that echoed through the stillness.

Sleep eluded me, my mind churning with thoughts of the future, of the battles yet to come. I lay awake, staring into the darkness, my heart pounding with a mixture of fear and determination.

As the first light of dawn crept through the cracks in the walls, I felt Riku stir beside me. We rose together, our bodies aching with the strain of the previous day's exertions.

But there was no time for rest, no time for weakness. We had a family to protect, a legacy to uphold. With renewed determination, we stepped out into the morning light, ready to face whatever challenges the new day might bring.

The sun cast a pale glow across the ruined landscape, illuminating the devastation that surrounded us. But in that moment, I felt a flicker of something else, a glimmer of hope that refused to be extinguished.

We were still alive, still fighting. And as long as we had each other, as long as we held fast to the love that bound us together, I knew that we would find a way to survive, to reclaim our rightful place among the living.

I watched as our children emerged from the dwelling, their eyes wide with a mixture of fear and curiosity. They had grown up in this harsh world, had known nothing but the constant threat of the undead. And yet, they still possessed a resilience that never ceased to amaze me.

Riku knelt down beside them, her voice soft but firm. "Stay close to us," she said, her eyes scanning the surrounding area for any signs of danger. "We have to be careful, but we also have to keep moving forward."

I nodded in agreement, my hand resting on the hilt of my sword. "We'll find a new place to call home," I said, my voice filled with a conviction I didn't quite feel. "A place where we can build a future for our children."

We set out across the barren landscape, our footsteps echoing in the eerie silence. The sun beat down upon us, a merciless reminder of the unforgiving nature of this new world.

But as we walked, I couldn't shake the feeling that we were being watched, that something sinister lurked just beyond the shadows. It was a feeling I had grown accustomed to, a constant companion in this life we had chosen.

We had to be vigilant, had to be ready for whatever challenges lay ahead. But even in the midst of this darkness, I found solace in the love that surrounded me, in the unbreakable bond that held our family together.

As we walked, I allowed myself a moment of reflection, a moment to remember all that we had lost, all that we had sacrificed. But I also allowed myself to dream, to imagine a future where our children could grow up without fear, where they could know the joys of a life untainted by the horrors of this world.

It was a dream that seemed impossible, a dream that teetered on the edge of madness. But it was a dream that I clung to, a dream that gave me the strength to keep putting one foot in front of the other, to keep fighting for the ones I loved.

The End.

Don't miss out!

Visit the website below and you can sign up to receive emails whenever Aaron Abilene publishes a new book. There's no charge and no obligation.

https://books2read.com/r/B-A-YOIP-DSKGF

BOOKS 2 READ

Connecting independent readers to independent writers.

Also by Aaron Abilene

505
505
505: Resurrection

Balls
Dead Awake
Before The Dead Awake
Dead Sleep
Bulletproof Balls

Carnival Game
Full Moon Howl
Donovan
Shades of Z

Codename
The Man in The Mini Van

Deadeye

Deadeye & Friends

Cowboys Vs Aliens

Ferris

Life in Prescott

Afterlife in Love

Tragic Heart

Island

Paradise Island

The Lost Island

The Lost Island 2

The Lost Island 3

The Island 2

Pandemic

Pandemic

Prototype

Prototype

The Compound

Slacker

Slacker 2

Slacker 3

Slacker: Dead Man Walkin'

Survivor Files

Survivor Files: Day 1

Survivor Files : Day 1 Part 2

Survivor Files : Day 2

Survivor Files : On The Run

Survivor Files : Day 3

Survivor Files : Day 4

Survivor Files : Day 5

Survivor Files : Day 6

Survivor Files : Day 7

Survivor Files : Day 8

Survivor Files : Day 9

Survivor Files : Day 10

Survivor Files : Day 11

Survivor Files : Day 12

Survivor Files : Day 13

Survivor Files : Day 14

Survivor Files : Day 15

Survivor Files : Day 16

Survivor Files : Day 17

Survivor Files : Day 18

Texas

Devil Child of Texas
A Vampire in Texas

The Author

Breaking Wind
Yellow Snow
Dragon Snatch
Golden Showers
Nether Region
Evil Empire

Thomas

Quarantine
Contagion
Eradication
Isolation
Immune
Pathogen
Bloodline
Decontaminated

TPD

Trailer Park Diaries
Trailer Park Diaries 2
Trailer Park Diaries 3

Virus

Raising Hell

Zombie Bride

Zombie Bride

Zombie Bride 2

Zombie Bride 3

Standalone

The Victims of Pinocchio

A Christmas Nightmare

Pain

Fat Jesus

A Zombie's Revenge

The Headhunter

Crash

Tranq

The Island

Dog

The Quiet Man

Joe Superhero

Feral

Good Guys

Romeo and Juliet and Zombies

The Gamer

Becoming Alpha

Dead West

Small Town Blues

Shades of Z: Redux
The Gift of Death
Killer Claus
Skarred
Home Sweet Home
Alligator Allan
10 Days
Army of The Dumbest Dead
Kid
The Cult of Stupid
9 Time Felon
Slater
Bad Review: Hannah Dies
Me Again
Maurice and Me
The Family Business
Lightning Rider : Better Days
Lazy Boyz
The Sheep
Wild
The Flood
Extinction
Good Intentions
Dark Magic
Sparkles The Vampire Clown
From The Future, Stuck in The Past
Rescue
Knock Knock
Creep
Honest John
Urbex
She's Psycho
Unfinished

Neighbors
Misery, Nevada
Vicious Cycle
Relive
Romeo and Juliet: True Love Conquers All
Dead Road
Florida Man
Hunting Sarah
The Great American Zombie Novel
Carnage
Marge 3 Toes
Random Acts of Stupidity
Born Killer
The Abducted
Whiteboy
Broken Man
Graham Hiney
Bridge
15
Paper Soldiers
Zartan
The Firsts in Life
Giant Baby

Milton Keynes UK
Ingram Content Group UK Ltd.
UKHW030912121124
451094UK00001B/112